KISSED BY AN ALIEN

Emily Michel

This is a work of fiction. Similarities to real people, places, or events are entirely coincidental.
KISSED BY AN ALIEN

MAGICAL

MOMENTS

This one is for the librarians.

Thank you for pointing me to the books I liked, the books I loved, the books I needed, and the books I had to read for some damn paper.

Thank you for never doubting I could read twenty books in three weeks, and for not judging me when I didn't.

And thank you for working against censorship. Keep fighting the good fight.

Author's Note

This book contains the following elements: explicit language, explicit sex scenes, mention of past domestic violence, law enforcement, mention of past parental death, and a brief description of blood.

I welcome comments on my website should you find something upsetting that was not mentioned above.

For a free short story, bonus content, updates on current and future projects, and early looks at covers, excerpts, and review copies, sign up for my Magical Musings Newsletter.

EmilyMichelAuthor.com/Newsletter

CHAPTER 1

Mere Played It Cool

"He's back," Dee said in a singsong voice.

Mere already knew. She always did. The hairs on her arms stood at attention and the air in the library seemed to thicken the moment he stepped foot inside. But admitting it to Dee would be unwise. As good as her intentions might be, the older woman would tease her mercilessly about landing such a "hunk."

Instead, Mere played it cool. "Oh?"

"How can you not notice…that?" Dee gestured in his direction.

She wasn't wrong. Long and lean with the tan of someone who worked outside all day, the newest arrival in Strawberry Creek was a man nearly every woman in town noticed. Married or not. Old and young. Even old Mrs. Murillo stared at him from behind the cart of books she was supposed to be re-shelving with a lusty gleam Mere hoped she still had at age eighty.

"Lots of people come through here, Dee. If I stop what I'm doing every single time, I'd never get anything done."

"If you never stop, never talk to anyone, how are you going to make friends? And he could be a very *special* kind of friend."

That was a doozy of a question, and she did not want to answer it in front of everyone in the freaking library. Enough people knew her past as it was—small towns were like that. But she didn't need to broadcast her history to tall, handsome strangers.

"I don't need new friends," she said instead.

Dee tsked and continued scanning in the returns from last night. The man approached, pulling out a wallet from his pocket. Mere stood and met him at the desk.

"Hi, there. How can I help you today, Mr. Haynes?"

He pushed his messy dark brown hair out of his face and smiled, and when it reached his pale blue eyes, they sparkled, hand to God.

"I told you, you can call me Anders," he said in a softly accented voice.

She hadn't been able to place the accent yet. He either studied English from a young age or had moved to the US long ago and lost what accent he had. It was only curiosity, as no one seemed to know much of anything about him. The only thing she knew that no one else did was his penchant for old town records.

"Yes, you have. I'm sorry. I'll try to remember next time." Mere returned the smile.

His eyes shone with an almost otherworldly brightness, pushing away the coldness she had glimpsed at first. She kept herself from swooning like a heroine in her favorite historical romances by sheer willpower. Holy cow.

"I'm looking for anything you have from 1920."

"In Strawberry Creek, or in the state?"

"Anything you have."

"Okay. Why don't you have a seat at a table? I'll dig around and bring you what I find."

"Thank you, Meretta."

A shiver threatened to overtake her upon hearing her name from his lips. She suppressed it but remained frozen in place as he walked to his favorite table in the corner of the library. She couldn't help but admire his loping stride and the way his muscles worked under his tight t-shirt and work jeans. Anders pulled out a chair, and it squealed horribly on the tile, breaking the spell. Before he could notice her slack-jawed gaping, she disappeared down the stairs to the musty archives.

The town of Strawberry Creek had only ten thousand permanent residents. It swelled in the summer by another couple thousand as the desert dwellers escaped the brutal heat. The library was on the first floor of the old town hall and doubled as the archives.

Anders Haynes had first stepped foot in her domain about a month ago, and as the newest resident, a hot one at that, he quickly became the talk of the town. Mere could see why. He rarely talked to anyone besides her. As far as she knew, he only came to the library and stopped by farm stands for fresh produce and meat.

Their conversations, near a dozen by now, had only been about the archives. He politely requested materials from a particular year, read them, stacked them neatly when he finished, and thanked her just as politely. Mere might be the envy of every woman in town, but she didn't know the man any better than they did.

The motion sensor turned on the lights as she moved deep into the stacks. She pulled the bound folios of the local newspaper first. They were the oldest available. The paper had been founded in 1920, and the city incorporated the year prior.

She moved to the other archive material. They still had some microfiche, though the machine was a bit touchy. Dee had been applying for grants to digitize them for almost a decade. This year's application had made it through the first round, so they were keeping their fingers crossed. If it didn't come through soon, Mere would have to think outside the box. Maybe a university student home for the summer might be willing to volunteer some time. Lord knew, neither she nor Dee had any to spare.

She put the film on top of the folios. There was a disintegrating scrapbook a town council member had assembled covering the entire decade. She added it to the pile. All that was left were the official minutes of council meetings, some blueprints, and a box of photos. Mere would have to make another trip if he wanted any of that.

Trudging up the steps, she bumped her hip against the crash bar and the door swung open, letting in the bright light of the library. Mere blinked, clearing the dust and waiting for her eyes to adjust. Her perfectly balanced pile tilted alarmingly, but she righted it before creating a scene. She carefully walked over to the table where Anders sat and plonked the stack in front of him.

"There's council minutes and blueprints if you want them."

He shook his head. "No. At least, not yet."

"What are you looking for?"

"Not sure, but I doubt it has anything to do with buildings. And minutes are too boring."

She chuckled, and he graced her with another smile that made his eyes twinkle. Like, really twinkle. It would be eerie if it wasn't so beautiful. Almost how a cat's caught the light in a dim room.

"Oh, there was a box of photographs. I couldn't balance it with everything else, but I don't mind getting it if you want."

"That is very kind of you. I'd appreciate it."

"Be right back."

She walked across the library floor. Mrs. Murillo watched her, as did the young moms, and one dad, sitting with their toddlers in story time. The green blanket of jealousy weighed

4

lightly upon her. They had nothing to be jealous about. She hardly knew the man.

Mere returned quickly with the box, and after yet another of his heart-shattering smiles, she resumed her regular duties. At 4:45, the alarm on her phone went off. Dee got ready for the pre-closing rush and Mere made the rounds, making sure the patrons knew they had only a few more minutes.

Anders stacked his pile neatly, as usual. "Do you need some help returning these?"

"Oh no, sorry. Employees only. It's no big deal."

"Well, thank you again. I'll see you soon."

Her heart did a strange pitty-pat at the thought of seeing him again.

Dee finished checking out the last patron, and Mere locked the door behind him as he left.

"I saw you making googly eyes at that excellent specimen of mankind." Dee waggled her eyebrows.

"I was not making googly eyes. I don't flirt."

"You should. Especially since you're the only person I've ever seen him smile at."

"No." She couldn't be. Anders was polite. Surely that wasn't true.

"Just calling it like I see it. Need some help with those?"

Mere gathered the archive material. "No, I got it. Your husband should be home today, right?"

He worked in the big city a couple hours away. The pay was great, better than he could do in a small town, but it meant spending the week away from his wife. It was only for a bit longer. He would retire in a year or two and be full-time in Strawberry Creek.

"Thanks, Mere." Dee picked up her purse and lunch sack with a wide smile.

"No worries."

Dee slipped out, and Mere took the first stack, leaving the

box of photos on the table. She put everything back where she found it and returned for the pictures. Then the screwy light downstairs decided the room was empty and went out. She missed the last step and stumbled, spilling the box of photos all over the floor. The light came back on and her only injury was a mildly bruised pride. At least no one had seen her.

She grabbed handfuls of the old photos of people likely long dead, except perhaps for the youngest, and dropped them in the box. One photo caught her eye, and she froze.

A familiar face stared back at her. It was a black-and-white picture, so she couldn't be certain those eyes were blue, but the hair was dark and the figure was tall and lean. And the smile fit Anders to a T.

CHAPTER 2

Mr. Leonard Reed

This couldn't be possible. The photo was a hundred years old, for goodness' sake. Anders wasn't over forty, at the oldest. But this man could be his twin.

The man who looked like Anders—or did Anders look like him?—stood in front of the old general store. The building had been demolished when she was a child. A hotel for summer visitors was more important than town history.

Mere turned the photo over. In neat but faded handwriting, the caption on the back read, "Mr. Leonard Reed, General Store proprietor, 1920."

Reed? Did she know any Reeds? She racked her brain. Hadn't there been a Jason Reed in her high school class? Maybe. It had been almost fifteen years since she graduated, and even then she was shy. She had her best friend, and a couple other trusted people to hang out with, and that was about it.

Maybe Anders was a long-lost relative. What were the other options? Vampire? Immortal? She wasn't living in some gothic novel. It was a coincidence, not a conspiracy. But Mere still slipped the photo into her cardigan pocket. She shouldn't have. It was against the rules. But her parents expected her for dinner at six, and she barely had enough time to get there if she left now. Otherwise, she would have to answer all sorts of questions.

Her parents worried. It made them good parents, she guessed, but she avoided answering their probing questions whenever possible. She worked tomorrow, and hopefully could find some spare minutes to research this Leonard Reed.

She shoved the box on its shelf and hurried up the stairs. The usually pleasant basement took on a more sinister air after discovering the possibility of an immortal being living in her town. Mere pushed away the flight of fancy. There was a logical explanation, she just had to find it. Vampires weren't real. And *Highlander* was only an old movie and TV show. No stranger was going to come looking for Anders Haynes's head.

Nevertheless, she hurried to her car and locked the doors as soon as she closed them. It had been a few years since she'd felt unsafe. Strawberry Creek was her home, and though she had only a few close friends, pretty much everyone in town knew her dad. It wasn't high tourist season, with more strangers than usual. Things were quiet, yet this situation spooked her.

Mere drove the speed limit, but she was on autopilot. Of course she was spooked. It wasn't normal to find a photo of a man long-dead who looked exactly the same as the living one she'd been helping over the past month. And fantasizing about, if she were being honest with herself.

She told Dee she hadn't noticed Anders. That was a flat-out lie. She couldn't help but notice him. He invaded her thoughts during the day, her fantasies at night. Mere was good at hiding her attraction, but this discovery disturbed her.

Pulling up in front of her parents' house, she killed the engine, took a deep breath, and prepared to enter. She loved her parents, she really did, but they knew and loved her, too.

Both excelled at picking out subtle clues something was wrong. They'd had a hell of a lot of practice when she was in high school, and the past few years had only reinforced it.

She put on her game face and got out of the car. The long-standing rule was family never knocked. Mere walked through the kitchen door to her parents sharing a passionate kiss.

"Ew."

"Well, how do you think you got here?" her mother asked with a laugh in her dark brown eyes.

Mere shared her mother's body type, but not much else. She inherited ash-blond hair from somewhere, but her dad had medium brown and her mother's was almost black. Her dad swears Aunt Nadine used to be blond, but Mere only knew her as a white-haired old lady (her words, not Mere's).

"I don't want the reminder."

She was mostly kidding. Her parents were sweet, and she once hoped to share what they had with someone special. She had even found that person. Or so she assumed. Turned out she was wrong, terribly, horribly wrong.

"Have a seat, sweetheart. Dinner's ready."

"Smells great."

She dropped her purse next to the kitchen door and sat at the dining room table. Looked like pasta salad and fruit for dinner tonight. Suited her just fine. She'd enjoyed these dinners since returning to Strawberry Creek, and her parents loved having her around. Her dad's cooking was great, and her mother made wonderful salads with a knack for picking out the best produce.

"So…what's up, hon?" her father asked halfway through dinner, peering at her with his hazel eyes. Hers were smack dab in between her parents, a hue best described by the tiger's eye gemstone.

"What do you mean?"

"You are an open book, Mere. Something's bothering you,"

her mother said.

Here they go.

In truth, she couldn't blame them. She'd been a mess when she first returned to town over five years ago. It had been six months before she started looking for work. And another year before she moved out. Mere still had her moments, but today it wasn't her past bothering her. It was her present.

She couldn't deny something was wrong. Her mother, the social worker, would scent the lie like a shark with blood in the water. And her father, the high school principal, was only slightly less astute. But she could tell a partial truth.

"Don't tell me you-know-who tried contacting you again." Her father's usually genial face grew stern, and she knew why all the kids at the high school spilled their guts to him the moment things went pear-shaped.

"No, I haven't heard from him in ages." Oddly, though, it still hurt to say his name. Or hear it. Or think it. She shoved it aside. Betrayal was never easy, but she had come to terms with it. "Just distracted by work."

"Work? I thought you loved it there." Her mother studied her, searching for signs of God knew what.

"I do, Mom. But every job has its stresses. Today was slightly more stressful than most." Which was putting it mildly, but until Mere had answers, she wasn't going to mention the mysterious Mr. Haynes to her parents. They'd take it all wrong.

"You should get used to hearing his name. It's been five years, and it's getting a bit ridiculous."

"I'd rather pretend it never happened. The sooner I can forget he ever existed, the better." Mere struggled to keep her tone polite. Her parents were only trying to help. Unfortunately, they never seemed to take the hint that, at least in this, she didn't want it.

"Some pagan religions believe naming a thing gives you power over it." Her father, who started his career as a history teacher, was a font of little-known facts. "It's been so long, it shouldn't be a big deal. Tyson shouldn't—"

Mere clapped her hands over her ears. She wanted to forget the biggest mistake of her life, but her damn parents, as well-meaning as they were, wouldn't let her. The mention of his name had her flashing back to the last time she saw him. Ugly, angry, vicious. If she never remembered his face again, it would be too soon.

"Stop, Rich." Her mother laid a hand on his arm. He clamped his jaws shut.

Mere rose and tossed her napkin on the table. "I never want to hear his name again. Not from you, not from anyone. I know it's unreasonable. I know you're trying to help, but stop, please."

She stomped to the kitchen and jerked her purse off the floor. "Thank you for dinner. I'm sorry I won't be staying to clean up. I'm tired."

Pushing out the door, she heard her mother's sobs. Guilt tore at her, but she had her boundaries and needed to stick to them.

"It's okay, Jodi." Her father's words cut off as the door slammed shut behind her.

Mere started the car with a vigorous twist and drove straight home.

CHAPTER 3
The Cabinet of Death

A Saturday in the off-season was always quiet. A couple of older volunteers and a teenager helped her reshelve books, check in returns, check out patrons, and answer questions about the computers and copiers. Dee had this Saturday off.

"I need to clean up the archives," she said to Mrs. Murillo. "I had to meet my parents for dinner last night and didn't properly refile the materials Mr. Haynes requested."

Mrs. Murillo smirked and winked knowingly. "You sure that's all that happened down there?"

The heat rose in Mere's face, damn her Scandinavian ancestors.

"Oh, I'm just teasing, dear. Go on with you. I'll knock if there's anything we can't handle."

There was nothing Mrs. Murillo couldn't handle. Before she retired to Strawberry Creek, she was a librarian herself. She came in twice a week to help out, and Mere enjoyed having her. She was a real lifesaver whenever Mere encountered a new problem.

Mere padded down the stairs, clutching her cardigan around

her in the chill air of the basement. The shadows cast by the automatic fluorescent lights still creeped her out. Fingering the old photo in her pocket, she headed right for the folios she had dumped last night. What had Anders Haynes been looking for? She flipped through the pages and scanned them. Surely, something would jump out at her.

Unfortunately, nothing did. Nothing in the old newspapers told her there was some conspiracy going on. At least, nothing that would have a 130-year-old man risk coming back to his hometown and being discovered.

Speaking of Leonard Reed...she went to the Cabinet of Death. There was nothing wrong with the cabinet, but it was filled with copies of all the death certificates filed since the town was founded. Filed first by year, then alphabetically, she had to make a choice. Should she begin with the year she knew the man had been alive, or should she make an assumption and skip a few decades to when he may have been old?

Mere was nothing if not methodical. She started with 1920 and worked her way up. An hour later, deep into the 60s, a knocking broke her out of her almost trance-like state. She ran up the stairs and met Mrs. Murillo.

"Sorry, Mere, but someone needs to pay a fine."

As the only paid employee of the library and archives working today, she was the sole person able to accept money from patrons. The transaction only took a few minutes.

"You must have left a big mess," Mrs. Murillo said.

"Oh, I got distracted by the folios. I couldn't help but glance through them."

Mrs. Murillo shook her head with a smile. "You were born to be a librarian. I'm so glad you returned to Strawberry Creek."

"Me too."

Few knew the whole story, and she hoped they never would. They closed at five, and Mere returned to the archives, feeling slightly guilty. She shouldn't. These were public records, available for the asking. And she knew them backward and forward. It wouldn't take much longer.

She flipped through the death certificates. There. She pulled it out and took it to the only desk at the far end of the room. Leonard Reed died of natural causes at the ripe age of eighty-five on January 18, 1974. He would have been thirty-one in 1920. That tracked.

Mere knew her obsession with this was ridiculous. She was making a mountain out of a molehill. Anders looked to be in his thirties, maybe a couple of years older than her. It was only a coincidence he resembled a man who died long before she'd been born. Or—and this was the most natural explanation— he was a distant relative whose passing resemblance was enhanced by the old photo and her overactive imagination.

After her experience with the asshat never to be named, she often doubted her own intuition. Maybe, just maybe, she was looking for a reason to put some distance between herself and Anders. The man was attractive, polite, and seemed to like her. Was it enough of a threat for her to create some ridiculous obstacle in her head?

Probably. The asshat had truly messed with her mind.

Mere pulled out the picture and studied it once more. She knew she should put it back, but some instinct made her tuck it into her pocket once more. She would ask her mom if she knew of Leonard Reed. Born and raised in Strawberry Creek, her mom had deep roots in the community. And if not, maybe her great-aunt would remember. She was in her eighties herself, but still sharp as a shark's tooth.

She locked up and drove home.

At least, she tried. A loud bang and a strange flopping sound had her pulling over about two miles from her little house. Her old Sentra had blown a tire. She rolled to a stop and put the damn thing into park.

Mere bent her head and lightly tapped it against the steering wheel. Why? This was the last thing she needed.

Getting out of the car, she clutched her sweater tightly around her and shoved her hands into the pockets. The rippled edge of the bothersome photo tickled her fingers. With a sigh, she circled her vehicle. The right rear tire was as flat as a pancake. She opened the glove box and pulled out the owner's manual. Mere had been lucky and only changed tires for practice as a teen and once…

Smoldering anger washed over her, but she pushed it away, as she'd done often the past five years. Anger wouldn't change her freaking tire.

She used the light in the trunk to read the instructions and pulled out the jack and tire iron. A green Chevy truck that had to be older than her by at least a decade but was in much better condition than her eight-year-old sedan, pulled in behind her. Clutching the iron tightly, Mere put on her don't-mess-with-me face. One would never describe it as mean, let alone aggressive, but she found it an effective deterrent when accosted by unknown men.

But this man wasn't unknown. Anders Haynes unfolded his body from the driver's seat. He pulled off his trucker cap and tossed it into the cab.

"I finally get to repay your kindness, Meretta."

"I appreciate it, Mr.—Anders, but I've got this under control."

After suspecting him of—what, exactly? Being the physical reincarnation of a man who died decades ago? That sounded bonkers even in her head. But it wasn't in her nature to accept help from strangers, especially since his royal asshatness.

"It will go faster with two. And those lug nuts have a tendency to get stuck. I have tools in my truck if that's the case."

The man made sense. She wasn't great getting her old beater into the shop for regular tire maintenance, no matter how many times her dad reminded her.

"Fine. But once the lug nuts are off…"

He held up his hands in surrender. "I will allow the damsel to rescue herself."

"Good. As long as we're on the same page."

His lips twitched into an almost smile.

They got to work. The nuts were, indeed, stuck tight. With his whipcord muscles and a liberal application of lubricant, Anders got them off much more quickly than Mere could have. But now the sun was near the horizon, casting strange shadows.

"Let me shed some light on the situation." He started the truck.

With the light and his help, the spare was on more quickly than it would have taken her alone. Of course, if Anders hadn't come to her rescue, she would have called her dad when she realized the nuts were stuck.

Awkwardly, Mere shoved her hands into her pockets again. "Thank you."

Another almost smile. "You are welcome. I am glad I was in the right place at the right time."

She kicked at the ground awkwardly. Mere's interactions with people outside of work or family over the last several years were limited, to say the least. She wasn't entirely sure what she was supposed to do next. Pulling out her hand, she offered it to him.

The photo fluttered to the ground. Anders picked it up before she could take a step toward it. She held her breath.

The man glanced at it, and his face grayed. "Where did you get this?"

CHAPTER 4

Just a Coincidence

"It fell out of a box the other day. Isn't it funny the guy looks so much like you?" Mere giggled nervously. What if she was wrong? What if something not quite human stood in front of her?

"Is that why you have it?"

His tone hadn't changed. Neither had his unnaturally still expression. Mere's heart raced and her palms grew slick with sweat. Part of her wanted to grab the photo out of his hand and run, never stopping. Another part watched him closely, waiting to see what happened next.

"Um, I forgot I had it." *Liar.*

God, she hated liars. She would have to discuss this with her therapist at her next appointment.

Anders peered at her, those blue eyes of his shining strangely in the dim light. He held out the photo, and she took it from him gingerly.

"Well, make sure it gets back to where it belongs. Who is it?"

The tension holding his body rigid seeped away, and Mere's body reacted in kind. *See, it was just a coincidence.*

"It says 'Leonard Reed' on the other side. A long-lost relative of yours?"

His shoulders shrugged sinuously, a wave of rippling muscles drawing her attention. How was he doing that? Mere bit her lip to keep from staring at him with mouth agape.

"My grandmother may have mentioned his name. Life is funny this way, is it not?"

"It's a small world," she said, pulling the old cliché out, dusting it off, and instantly regretting the boring response. She was remarkably out of practice.

A grin flashed across his lips, and his eyes sparked with...something. Not the wariness of a moment ago, but something that looked a lot like interest.

"Yes, this world is very small."

"I have dinner to cook, so I'd best get going. Thank you again."

Anders looked at his toes and took a deep breath. "I'd like to buy you dinner."

Oh. *Oh.* The dawning realization that perhaps he hadn't been coming to the library for only the archives hit her in the solar plexus, making speech impossible. It had been so long. The few men her age she knew in Strawberry Creek were taken. And she hadn't been able to trust anyone, including herself, since she escaped the dickhead five years ago.

"Sure, but not tonight." The words were out of her mouth before she could bite her tongue to keep from uttering them. Dammit.

He rubbed the back of his neck and shuffled his feet in the dirt, sending a rock skittering into the road.

"I promised my great-aunt I'd cook for her tonight. I'm off the next two days. Do you want to meet at Fielding's tomorrow at six?"

What the hell? It was as if her mouth had a mind of its own. It was all true. Aunt Nadine looked forward to her visits. And though her aunt wouldn't mind at all getting dumped in favor of a hot guy, Mere wanted to ask her about Leonard Reed. But she'd said yes. Like a woman who flirted with men. Like a woman who dated. Like a woman who hadn't fled an asshole abuser.

Anders's smile returned, bigger than ever. It lit his entire face and made him even hotter, if that was possible.

"I accept. I will see you tomorrow at six. Drive safely, Meretta."

He strode to his truck and hopped in. Mere got into her car, started it, and drove away. He waited until she pulled onto the road before turning around and driving in the opposite direction. Had he come to find her? Had he been following her? Or had he merely gone out of his way to help a damsel in a modicum of distress?

These thoughts plagued her all the way home.

Mere dumped her stuff on the table in the hall and hurried over to the other side of the duplex. In exchange for checking on her aunt daily and helping with errands and doctors' appointments, she lived in half the duplex for well below market rent. Nadine got company, her parents got a little freedom, and Mere got affordable rent on a small-town librarian's salary.

"Sorry, Auntie Nay, blew a tire."

Her aunt putzed in the kitchen, putting together a salad.

"Oh no! Everything okay?"

She peered through her thick lenses with a wide grin. Despite her downy snow-white hair, she was not a feeble old woman, something she constantly reminded Mere's parents of. It was an old argument, but when Mere had moved back, they found a reasonable solution.

"Obviously." Mere chuckled.

Nadine clicked her tongue. "Don't get sassy with me, young lady."

She didn't mean it. There was nothing in this world Nadine appreciated more than a sassy young woman.

Mere planted a kiss on her aunt's cheek and pulled out the ingredients for dinner. She put on a pot of water for the spaghetti and grabbed the container of thawed sauce.

"Does it even count if I just reheat your leftovers?" Mere dumped the sauce into another pot.

"It's your company I appreciate, not whether you cook. Plus, who else am I going to pass the recipe down to?"

Aunt Nadine placed the salad on the table along with her favorite Italian dressing. She sliced the bread while they waited for the water to boil and the sauce to warm. Handing Mere a large hunk, she sat at the table and spread a generous portion of butter all over her piece. Mere joined her.

"Ramona's?" she asked around a heavenly mouthful.

"Of course. How was your day?"

She swallowed. Mere was more honest with Nadine than with her own parents. Her aunt was one of those women who assumed you were as capable as she until proven otherwise. Instead of hovering, waiting for the breakdown, Nadine was always willing to listen, always willing to help pick her up off the floor, brush herself off, and get back to living. It meant more to her than she could ever say.

"Interesting." She wiped her hands off on the paper napkin and pulled out the photo of Leonard Reed. "I found this yesterday. Do you remember him?"

Mere passed the picture to her aunt. Nadine lifted her chin to position the bifocals for a better look. She flipped it over and read the name. A wistful smile grew upon her lips, and she stroked her long braid, which hung over a shoulder.

"Yes, Mr. Reed. I remember him. He was the mayor not too long after this was taken, if I remember right. Before I was born, anyway. Volunteered with the fire department and got elected to the school board, too. That was when I was in high school. Dated his nephew for a few months before I met Sergio."

"What was he like?"

Nadine returned the picture. "Why do you want to know about some old codger who died long before you came around to light up this old lady's world?"

Mere licked her lips. She didn't want to lie to Nadine. Hell, she wasn't sure she *could* lie to her aunt. The woman was people smart.

"He has a captivating face." Even more so, seeing one so close to it on Anders.

"Got a crush on a dead man, huh?" Nadine smiled wickedly. Mere could almost tell the instant she put the pieces together. She should have kept her damn mouth shut. "Or not so dead. It strikes me that Mr. Reed looks an awful lot like a certain newcomer who I ran into a time or two at the library."

The blood rushed to her cheeks, and Mere got up to check the water, hiding the flush. She tossed in salt and the pasta, and after giving herself a moment to calm down, rejoined her aunt at the table.

A puzzled expression replaced the wicked gleam in Auntie Nay's eyes.

"What is it?" Mere asked.

"It's a bit odd, but if I recall the gossip correctly"—Nadine always recalled the gossip correctly—"I swear I heard the new hottie in town had rented the old Reed place out in the county."

CHAPTER 5

The World Flirt in Town

Mere's dreams were filled with strange beings chasing her, and Anders's bright blue eyes shining from each face she encountered. She woke with an overwhelming sense of dread.

The coincidences were piling up. Anders could be Mr. Reed's much younger twin, and now he lived where Mr. Reed had. But what did she believe was going on? Vampires weren't real, plus she had seen him on a bright, sunny day. No sparkles, no dust, no bursting into flames, and no ugly magical daylight jewelry. No stranger had come to town with a big-ass sword and proclaimed there could be only one survivor. That would have inserted itself into local lore. Which left a Benjamin Button effect; somehow, Mr. Reed was aging backward. None of those things were remotely possible. Coincidence was all that remained.

Dread pooled into a rock in her gut as the day went on. Mere had a date with him tonight. She should cancel, but she didn't have his number. Or an email. What had she been thinking? She could stand him up, but her curiosity won out, helped along by her distinct trust issues.

If Anders wasn't who he said he was, she needed to know. The last time she trusted someone, she had been hurt, both physically and emotionally. She'd be damned if she would let that happen again.

Mere put on her prettiest blouse and her most flattering jeans. She curled her ash-blond hair and did her make-up, picking the subtle browns to highlight her eyes. A spritz of her favorite perfume and she was out the door, dressed to impress. This would either be an excellent first date or a disaster of extraordinary proportions.

She pulled into Fielding's parking lot precisely at six. Though her little car looked like a piece of crap, it was as reliable as Old Faithful. Nothing seemed to stop it from getting from place to place, with the rare exception of a blown tire. After visiting the website of the tire place first thing this morning, she scheduled an appointment for tomorrow. It was nice having Mondays off.

There he was, waiting in front of the restaurant. The string lights around the porch lit him like some leading man in an old movie. He looked off into the distance, but as she approached, he stilled for an instant before turning slowly. Once again, his eyes seemed to glow.

Mere walked up the steps, and his smile greeted her. An answering one formed on her own lips, as though her body was happier to see him than her mind.

"You look lovely, Meretta."

Unlike all the other people in her life, Anders insisted on using her full name, and it sent a shiver along her spine every time.

"Thanks. You look…"

He looked about the same as always, dressed in jeans, cowboy boots, and a neat button-down shirt. The boots had been brushed clean, and the jeans were newer and darker than what he wore to the library.

"About the same," she finished. Ugh, could she be any more awkward? "But that's good. You look good."

His smile widened and some tension left his shoulders. "You do not date often?"

"That obvious?"

He nodded but kept his mouth shut. Perhaps he was a wiser man than most.

"Well, it's your lucky day! You have a date with the worst flirt in town, who will undoubtedly do something incredibly embarrassing by the end of the night."

A low chuckle erupted from him and sent a wash of heat through her body. "When you put it that way, my expectations for the evening just became more…imaginative."

He held open the door for her, and as she passed, the air crackled between them. Mere desperately wanted to touch him, brush against him, to see what would happen. She restrained herself, but the look on his face, half surprise and half a darker and more dangerous emotion, told her she wasn't the only one holding back.

A hunger having nothing to do with food came over her. Mere hadn't felt this way in a very long while.

"Table for two?" the maître d' asked. Her mouth formed a little O of recognition as she looked from Mere to Anders, Great, the rumor mill would send word to her parents before they could hear it from the horse's mouth. Mere wouldn't hear the end of it.

"Yes, thank you." Anders stood directly behind her, close enough for his body heat to travel the few inches and warm her from head to toe, and all the other places in between.

"Right this way." Her voice held a knowing smirk, though her face remained pleasantly neutral. Or maybe Mere was reading too much into this.

She led them to a booth in the far corner, away from the other diners, where they would have privacy. Anders slid into one side and Mere into the other. The maître d' left their menus in front of them and slipped away. An uncomfortable silence descended. Mere picked up her menu to increase the emotional and visual distance.

"What do you recommend here?" Anders asked, not bothering with the menu.

She peeked over hers to find him studying her. Captivated by his shining eyes, she forgot what he'd asked for a moment. He blinked, and the memory came flooding back.

"Everything is good here," she whispered, her voice husky. Why was her voice husky? They were out for dinner in public. *In public*, she reminded her body.

"What is your favorite?" Another fierce spark flickered through the depths of his eyes. He was as still as a predator stalking its prey, yet Mere felt as safe as she ever had before she'd left for college.

Her mouth went dry and her voice stopped working. Mere licked her lips, praying her voice wouldn't betray her.

"Scampi."

There was something feral about his smile and the way he drank her in. Her heart thudded, and her imagination drifted to things that were not polite to think of in public. What was it about him? She hadn't reacted to a man this way, ever. Not even he who shall remain nameless.

"Then that is what I will have." Anders placed the menu to the side and turned his complete attention to her.

Apparently, his complete attention was even more of an aphrodisiac than his only slightly distracted attention. How had she never seen this from him before? He'd been to the library at least ten times in the past month, and all he displayed was polite interest. But now, with the force of his gaze, the presence behind those blue eyes, and the hungry look he wore all focused on her, strange feelings coursed through her. Feelings she had kept at bay for years.

Their server came over and did a double take. Yes, the mousy librarian out with the new hottie in town was cause for many raised eyebrows. The young man introduced himself and asked for their order.

"Meretta recommends the scampi," Anders said.

"It is excellent. Is that what you want, too?"

Mere hadn't even looked at the menu, using it as a shield against Anders's scrutiny.

"Yes, please." She handed the menu over like a woman in a trance.

"And two glasses of chardonnay, please," Anders said.

"Of course."

The server left, taking whatever armor she had against the beautiful man in front of her.

CHAPTER 6
Little Miss Awkward

Say something. Say anything. Stop looking like little miss awkward.
But Mere couldn't. Every time she tried to speak, the words left her head like dandelion fluff on a windy day. It seemed she was going for some record as the worst first date. Maybe it would make a good anecdote someday. Maybe she could post it to the awkward first date sub-Reddit.

"This is where you grew up?" Anders broke the silence when it stretched to an uncomfortable level.

She nodded, and he waited, his entire body still and calm with no evidence of impatience. She sipped her water and suddenly the words came.

"Yep. I was even Homecoming Queen my junior year."

"That's not only in movies and TV?"

Mere reminded herself of his accent. If he grew up outside the US, he might have no idea what a homecoming was.

"It's real. It was a big deal at the time, but now, it's a fun memory."

"Ah, so did you get a crown, like Miss America?"

"Yes, and my mom still has it in a box somewhere." She met

his gaze, worried he'd think it vain and trivial, but the corners of his lips ticked up and only curiosity filled his expression. Mere let the tension go and tore the bandage off. "I was born in the town hospital when we had one. My mom is a social worker for the county and my dad taught for years and is now the high school principal. We're a small family. My mom was raised by her aunt, Nadine, and my dad's folks died a year or two after he graduated from college. His older brother lives on the East Coast, and we only see him every couple of years."

"Your Aunt Nadine lives here. You cook for her."

How did he—? Oh, yeah, last night. "She lives in one half of a duplex, I live in the other. I try to cook for her once or twice a week. She doesn't need much help, but it's nice to cook for someone else. How about you? You said your grandmother mentioned Leonard Reed."

A coolness washed over him, and a mask dropped into place. This disinterested front was scarier than whatever hunger had greeted her earlier.

"I believe he was her uncle. I only know someone from my family lived here in Strawberry Creek. When I looked for a place to settle, I decided this would be nice."

"It's a little out of the way."

A strange look, halfway between wry amusement and anger, flitted over his face.

"I prefer being out of the way."

"My aunt says you moved into the old Reed place." She took a sip of her water.

"That is the only thing I do not appreciate about being out of the way. News travels fast in a small place."

Mere snorted in agreement. "Yeah, my parents will find out about our date before I call them tonight."

"Is that a bad thing?" From the way he leaned forward and the intensity of his gaze, he was honestly curious.

"No, it's just how it is. They worry about me and will be

28

disappointed I didn't tell them beforehand."

"But you are not a child anymore. Why would they worry so for you?"

"As my mom always says, I'm their child, and a mom never stops worrying."

She didn't mention how the last time she dated, things had gone so horribly wrong.

"That is not the way I was raised."

"America, the home of the helicopter parent." She shrugged with a chuckle. He joined in, the sound of it heating long-dormant places inside her.

Their server delivered their dinner. It smelled divine, rich with garlic and herbs. She was about to take a bite when she remembered how much garlic was in a good scampi. Too late now, and wasn't it okay as long as both parties had garlic?

Wait, was she planning on kissing this man? Her brain definitely needed to have a discussion with her body before making those kinds of decisions. But kissing Anders wouldn't be her worst idea this decade.

"Thank you for the recommendation," he said. "This is excellent."

"Glad to be of service." She promptly blushed. Dammit, why did her libido drag her thoughts deep into the gutter? She tried a different tactic. "I've talked a lot about me. Why don't you tell me about you?"

"There's not much to tell. I came to the US as an adolescent, moved around a lot. Now I'm here."

That wasn't helpful. In fact, it raised a red flag. Mr. Asshat had kept a lot of details about his life from her. She assumed he was a decent human being, and it turned out he was anything but. She wasn't getting the same vibes off Anders. Her ex had lied to her in order to keep things from her, keep her under his control. Anders just wasn't telling her things. Maybe he had his reasons. After all, this was only their first conversation about something other than dusty old records, but a brick in her wall slid back into place.

"What about your family?" she asked.

A hint of sorrow dimmed his bright eyes. "My parents are long dead, and I never had siblings."

"I'm sorry."

He made a small gesture of dismissal. "It was a long time ago. I have grieved and made my peace."

"Still, it's hard to be all alone."

Curiosity pushed aside the sadness. "It sounds like you speak from experience."

Mere raised her shoulders, hunching them into a defensive posture. She forced herself to relax. He had no way of knowing.

As he noted the motion, the smile disappeared, and his fingers curled into a loose fist on the table. "I'm sorry, it is not my business, but a kind person like you feeling lonely offends me."

She flinched when he'd clenched his fist, but his words put it into context. He wasn't mad at her, but at whoever had hurt her. The warmth that had been building all night blossomed into a bonfire.

"No, it's...it's okay. It was a while ago. I went away to college and stayed in the big city for a few years after. I made some decisions that put some distance between me and my family. It was lonely for a while. I came home five years ago, and things are better now."

It was lonely because Tyson had wanted her isolated. He put the walls between her and her family, as small as it was, as tight knit as it was. Tyson, who milked her for every last cent she earned before he made her his punching bag. When she finally screwed up the courage to leave, the dirtbag had driven to Strawberry Creek and threatened her family. He hadn't seen Nadine's baseball bat coming. Dude spent a night in the hospital with a concussion, then a few nights in jail while Mere got a restraining order in place. She hadn't seen him since. It helped that the sheriff had been her dad's student once upon a time.

"I didn't mean to bring up a delicate subject." He relaxed his hand.

Oddly, remembering the whole situation with Tyson in Anders's presence was far more comfortable than expected.

"It's not a big deal anymore. I'm here, back with my family, and I have a job I love." She took a long sip of her wine, which perfectly complemented the scampi.

"It is good to have work you love. Did you find anything else out about the photo?"

"The one of Mr. Reed?"

"Yes."

Since Leonard Reed was likely his relative, and was long dead anyway, she filled him in.

"You say he died almost fifty years ago?" Anders toyed with his half-eaten food.

"At eighty-five. He lived a long life and seemed well-respected. His obituary was truly gracious."

Anders nodded, almost as if agreeing with her. But he couldn't know. Mr. Reed was long dead before either of them had been born.

"That is what my grandmother said. Did you see anything about his will?"

His will? What an odd thing to ask. Although public record, wills seemed personal to her in a way a death certificate did not. And many people died without a will, anyway. Even if she looked, all she might find was dust and some wasted time.

"No. I didn't think to look. I can, if you want."

Why had she offered? Perhaps it was her curiosity, perhaps it was her insatiable need to help, perhaps it was her undeniable attraction to this man.

"I would appreciate it. I am wondering if there is any family

I might still contact. Perhaps they would want to know they have a distant relative in town."

"I went to school with a Reed but haven't heard anything about him in a long time. I can talk to my aunt. She remembered Mr. Reed, and there isn't a soul in this town she can't find."

Anders's face lit up like a fireworks show. "Perhaps I could speak to her sometime."

Oh, Auntie Nay would absolutely love that. A conversation with the newest hottie in town, one who had dated her great-niece, and someone she hadn't known for several presidencies. Fresh meat.

"Would you like to come over now?"

Had those words just come out of her mouth? She took some covert deep breaths to fight the flush threatening to migrate from her chest to her cheeks.

"Uh, are you sure I won't keep her up?"

"No. Nadine has always been a night owl."

"That is very kind of you. I don't know what I would do without you, Meretta."

Those weren't the first time she heard those words. They were the first words out of Tyson's mouth whenever she came crawling back. And she never truly believed them. If he cared so much, he never would have hit her in the first place. But between the gleam in Anders's eyes, the sincere set of his mouth, and his relaxed, non-threatening posture, she believed him, one thousand percent. Crap.

CHAPTER 7
The Yellow Sticky Note

Mere drove home slowly, and the lights of Anders's old truck flared in her rearview mirror.

Was she really bringing a man home? Even if it was to introduce him to Aunt Nadine, this was a big step for her. There was something about this man that made her trust him. It had nothing to do with him being as hot as any A-list actor, nor with him being the stereotypical handsome stranger who rescued a damsel in distress. Nothing at all.

She pulled into the driveway, and Anders parked on the street. Mere waited on the steps. Only once she got to Nadine's door did she notice her aunt's half of the duplex was dark and silent. Usually, she watched old movies until the wee hours of the morning, the flickering lights informing anyone wandering by that Nadine was in.

"Everything okay?" Anders asked, hands in his pockets and head tilted to the side.

Mere glanced at her own door. With her anxiety from sort of, kind of inviting a man over, she hadn't seen the yellow paper sticking there. She snatched it off the door.

Ramona rescued me from another night of Humphrey Bogart and insisted I come with her to the casino. Home tomorrow after lunch. Hope the date went well.

Ramona had chosen this night to take Nadine to the casino. Right. It was entirely conceivable her aunt had made the call and conveniently blamed it on her BFF. The wily old woman had cleared the way for a little extra privacy.

"Yes, but Nadine's not here. She and a friend took off to the casino."

"These things happen. Another time?"

His eyes glittered brightly in the dim porch light, his mouth tugged up into the barest smile, and a softness settled into the planes of his face. Mere leaned in, ready to apologize for wasting his trip, but her voice caught in her throat. For the first time in five years, she wanted to kiss someone. Not just someone, this man with kindness in his eyes and quiet strength in his body.

Slick fire flared between them. Anders reached out, but hesitated, his hand frozen halfway to her. Mere closed the distance, and his hand finished its journey, cupping her cheek as though her movement had unlocked something within him.

"I would very much like to kiss you, Meretta." His thumb made circles on her cheek and sent tendrils of pure lust to her core.

"Yes."

He lowered his head ever so slowly, as though afraid of spooking her. Once again, she closed the distance, standing on her tiptoes and shutting her eyes. His soft lips met hers and that slippery heat rippling between them earlier shot straight through the shields she'd built after Tyson, destroying them in an instant.

A low groan rumbled from his throat. Anders dropped his

hand to encircle her waist and pulled her tight against his hard, lean body. An answering moan escaped her, and the edges of his mouth quirked up into a grin. He broke away, taking a piece of her with him.

"I should go." His voice was husky with need, and those eyes—oh, how they gleamed in the night, shining like stars in the sky.

"No, stay."

Mere should have been surprised to hear those words come out of her mouth, but she wasn't. It seemed inevitable, from the first day he'd strolled into the library, the first time he meticulously pronounced her name, the first time their eyes had met. This man could be her destiny, if she let him, if she trusted him for one night. She let go of the past and lived in this moment.

Stepping away—the anguish of being more than inches from him threatened her newfound confidence—she unlocked her door and dragged him in by the arm.

His lips were on hers again as soon as the door clicked shut. His hands skimmed over her curves, sending shivers of delight and desire coursing through her. She pulled up his shirt and slid her palms over his back. His muscles twitched under her fingers and another groan rumbled through him.

He brought his hands around to her front and undid the buttons on her blouse, letting his fingers graze the exposed flesh. It was almost too much for her. Little fireworks kept going off in her peripheral vision, her knees threatened to collapse, and her breathing resembled panting more than anything else. Her panties were definitely wet, and she forced herself to slow down to enjoy this.

Taking a couple of fortifying breaths, she snagged him by the belt and pulled him to her bedroom. His low laugh filled the otherwise silent house, and she smiled in response. He pulled his shirt out of his jeans and unbuttoned it, tossing it to the side before they reached her room. Anders slid her blouse off her shoulders and cupped her breasts through her bra. Thank God she wore her best one tonight.

"You are beautiful." His face filled with wonder, and his fingers caressed the soft skin above the lace, sending jolts of desire through her body until they pooled low in her belly.

"Look who's talking." Mere let her gaze rove over his chest while her hands smoothed his rock-hard abs. What was this Adonis doing in her bedroom?

It didn't matter. They both wanted to be here. She would appreciate this for as long as it lasted. *Please let it last a long time.*

He unsnapped her jeans with a practiced flick and pulled them down, kneeling in front of her. Anders held the material as she stepped out of it, feeling exposed in her bra and panties. Goosebumps rose all over, but she wasn't sure if it was from the cool room or the heat in his gaze. Maybe both.

Standing, he pulled her in close and kissed her once more, banishing the goosebumps. Damn, she couldn't get enough of him. He could kiss her like this all night long and she would count it as time well spent. But she wanted more.

Mere's fingers trailed across his body before she unbuckled his belt, then unbuttoned his jeans. A growl thrummed in his chest, but his smile stayed firmly planted, one that should have sent her running with all-the-better-to-eat-you vibes. A deep-seated hunger lingered in his gaze, and she felt beautiful and wanted. He kissed her again, and her bra joined her other clothes. Anders broke the kiss and pulled his jeans and boxers down, freeing a substantial erection.

She gasped at this evidence of his blatant desire. Her panties grew even wetter. A thought, unwanted but important, hit her. It had been five years and this had happened so quickly.

"I-I don't have any, um, protection."

"I have learned it is always best to be prepared." He knelt and rummaged in his pockets, pulling out a condom with a triumphant flourish.

"Like a Scout?"

A wicked, wolfish smile crossed his lips as he stalked toward her. Mere backed up until her legs hit the bed, heart thudding, and an equally wicked smile grew on her lips.

"Something like that."

With a small push from him, she fell onto the bed. In a smooth motion, he knelt between her legs and removed her panties. He dragged his fingers up her leg and hesitated at the juncture of her thighs.

"I want to kiss you here." The lightest brush across her mound.

"Yes, please."

The grin widened briefly before disappearing altogether. His lips found her clit and sucked gently. Her hips bucked, and he laid his arm across her belly, holding her firmly in place. Heat and electricity shot through her with every swipe of his tongue. A heavy weight grew, filling her with warmth, until it exploded, and she drifted on a haze of pure pleasure.

Anders kissed his way up her body until his lips found hers again. He lingered on the kiss, delving deep into her mouth with his tongue, tasting her again. The hardness of his cock pressed against her thigh, and she wanted nothing more than to take the glorious length of him deep inside.

This time, she broke the kiss and wrapped her fingers around his cock. "More, please."

He hissed in a breath and bucked his hips as she worked her hand up and down. The little foil packet ripped. She let go and he slid the condom on. Mere scooted back on the bed and he knelt over her.

"Like this?" he asked, entwining his fingers with hers.

"Yes."

Anders slid into her, filling her in just the right way. She locked her legs around his waist as he rocked back and forth, and the warmth in her belly grew again. Mere glided her palms over his muscular back, and another groan escaped him. He brought his lips to hers, claiming them as they exploded together. Lost in the hazy afterglow, she snuggled into his embrace. The last thing she remembered was the warmth of her blankets covering her.

CHAPTER 8
Irresponsibly Dull Knives

The smell of coffee woke her, strong and bitter and warm. Anders walked in carrying two mugs, a lazy smile turning up the corners of his mouth. Oh, and what that mouth had done to her last night. The heat rose in her cheeks.

"I brought coffee, but if you want something else..." His voice was low with desire.

"Coffee, then we'll talk. Or something else."

He chuckled and handed over the brew. Black, just as she liked it. Sipping her mug, Mere took a moment to appreciate how good Anders looked sitting shirtless on her bed. Perhaps they wouldn't make it out of the bedroom. Wait, what time was it?

A glance at her clock told her she didn't have long to enjoy Anders's company before she needed to leave. Her appointment at the tire place was in a little over an hour.

Her thoughts must have appeared on her face because the smile left his.

"What is it?"

"I have an appointment to get a new tire this morning. I'm

afraid 'something else' is off the table."

"I certainly do not wish for you to postpone your appointment. Rescuing damsels in distress is exhausting."

She threw her pillow in his direction. He grinned and leaned in to kiss her, long and slow. The taste of the coffee mingled with the taste of him. It was one of the best things she'd ever experienced.

"I will make breakfast while you get ready," he said.

Mere was tempted to invite him to join her in the shower. She opened her mouth to say the words, but almost as though he could read her mind, his ice-blue eyes flared with heat. There was no way she would be on time for her appointment if she did what she so wanted to do.

Instead, she simply replied, "Thank you."

The fire in his eyes dimmed, but the lazy smile resurfaced. "You are most welcome."

Twenty minutes later, she emerged freshly washed, hair pulled into a ponytail, and dressed in jeans and a T-shirt. Anders stood next to her stove, scrambling eggs and buttering toast.

"I hope this works for you." His gaze raked her from head to toe.

"I love scrambled eggs and toast."

He flashed a quick grin and returned to his task. Mere poured them more coffee and glasses of cranberry juice and sat at the table. Anders had found her last avocado and a cutting board. He turned off the stove and sliced into the avocado.

She was about to warn him the knife was dull when he said, "Shit."

He grabbed a paper towel. Just her luck. Her new lover cut himself on her irresponsibly dull knives. She'd been meaning to take them over to the hardware store and get them professionally sharpened.

She trotted to the junk drawer, pulled out the first aid kit she stored there, and rushed to his side.

"I am fine. It is a little cut."

"Don't be a baby. Let's get it cleaned up."

Before he could protest, she grabbed his hand. Huh, it seemed he got some avocado in the wound. She tugged him to the sink, turned on the water, and shoved his finger under the stream.

He tried to jerk his hand away, but the green stuff kept coming. It oozed out and paled in the water, just like—

Mere dropped his hand and jumped back. "What the hell?"

His blood was green. Green! Who had green blood? Who?

The possibilities rushed through her brain, all the monster movies she'd ever seen, all the modern vampire and werewolf books she'd read, and then it caught on an idea. Green-blooded Vulcan. Alien. *Alien?*

Anders calmly—too calmly, in Mere's estimation—turned off the water and picked up the bandage. He wrapped it around the cut and took a deep breath before facing her. He took no steps toward her, which was good. If he came any closer, she was out of here. She glanced at the doorway, which led to the living room, and from there it was a straight shot to the front door. She could be outside and in her car in seconds. But were aliens faster than humans?

Aliens. Holy crap.

"I mean you no harm, Meretta. In fact, I had no intention of getting romantically involved with anyone while I was in town, but here we are."

She licked her lips. Not only was there an alien in her kitchen, but she had slept with him last night. Thank God they'd used condoms.

"What—"

"You are a highly intelligent woman. You have guessed what I am." He leaned against the counter and stared at her toes. If she made a run for it, she might have a chance. "My parents were on a scientific mission with a dozen others, and I was onboard to learn, a school holiday of sorts common with my people. The ship was damaged traversing the asteroid belt and crashed."

"School?"

"I was an adolescent, and it was customary to learn on the job. Before we enrolled in what you would consider high school, we tried out different jobs. See what we might be interested in, so we could focus our studies appropriately. Usually, you began with your parents."

He'd been a kid when his ship crashed. But when? Surely a UFO falling from the sky would make the news.

"Were you the only survivor?"

Staring at his clasped hands, he spoke in a monotone. "I am now. Several survived the initial crash, but the military arrived as we tried to salvage what we could from the ship. My parents grabbed me and ran. The soldiers caught us a hundred miles from here. My parents made me promise to survive, hid me, and sacrificed themselves to save me."

Mere's hand went to her heart without conscious effort. The poor kid he used to be.

"I'm sorry. That must have been terrifying."

Alone on an unknown, hostile world. Anders was a brave man.

"It was. Then I stumbled upon kind Mr. Reed. He took me in, allowing me to hide in the barn until the hullabaloo died down."

"But Mr. Reed died in the seventies. How old are you?"

"My best guess is about eighty of your years. But in my culture, I would still be considered in my prime. Mr. Reed must have died within a couple of years after I left."

Eighty. Dear lord, Talk about a May-December romance.

At no point in their discussion had he made a move toward her. His voice was even, almost clinical. And other than lie to her about who he was, he'd done nothing to show her he meant to hurt her. Mere let go of some of the tension in her body. She leaned against the counter behind her, mimicking his posture.

"What's with the green blood?"

At her question, he finally lifted his gaze to hers. A quick grin flashed across his lips. He stayed where he was, but a tiny bit of the tension filling the room evaporated.

"Symbiotic algae to help move oxygen around our bodies."

Mere wasn't a scientist. Hell, she'd struggled with science in high school and took the easiest science classes she could to earn her degree. But algae was a plant, and plants gave off oxygen, so it made a kind of logical sense.

"That's weird."

He shrugged and a little more tension left his posture. "No weirder than an iron-based molecule. Evolution can only use whatever resources are available. For humans, it was iron. For the Qilffir, it was algae."

She looked him over. "You look human. You act human. If evolution can only use whatever resources available, how come you look so much like us?"

His lips thinned and his body stiffened once more. "My people have a natural camouflage ability, usually to change color and blend into the background, but we created a device that uses DNA to give us the appearance of a native species. It's skin deep but has helped our scientists study sentient and near-sentient species across the galaxy. Since we shared a similar body type, Mr. Reed agreed I could use his DNA to blend in. It is one reason I am here. I would prefer not to return to my homeworld still looking like a human."

Mere bit her lip and studied his still-bare feet. "So, do you have tentacles or horns or scales?"

Anders chuckled. "Our species are not very different. I do have scales, but they are soft like a gecko's and more of an aqua due to the algae. No horns, no tentacles. Sorry to disappoint."

She didn't know if she was disappointed or not. Mere tried to picture Anders as an aqua lizard man, and the image that popped into her head had her covering her mouth so she wouldn't laugh. It wasn't polite to laugh at someone's natural skin color under any circumstances, but this entire situation was ridiculous. She had slept with an honest-to-God alien, and it may have broken her brain.

"I'm sorry. I don't mean to laugh, I really don't. It's just been too much."

"It is okay. It has been so long since I have seen myself as I once was, the idea seems absurd to me, as well."

Absurd—the understatement of the century. Something he'd said wormed its way into her consciousness. He was planning to return home. The idea he would soon leave took away any further desire to laugh, which was even more absurd. She'd known him a month, yet the idea of him leaving left a gaping hole in her heart.

Great, Mere, once again you fall fast for the wrong guy.

"You're leaving soon. Why?"

"I have spent the past several decades learning how to build a spaceship and earning the money to do so. I am missing two components. The navigation system and the DNA modifier, both of which I left with Mr. Reed. I did not understand exactly how old he was when I left here and decided later it might be safer if I never returned."

He met her gaze squarely and determination was written all over him, from the bold posture to the clenched jaw to the furrowed brow.

"What changed your mind?"

Anders tucked his thumbs into his pockets. "If I waited for the components to be available on the free market, I might be as relatively old as Mr. Reed was. My best shot at seeing my home planet again is to find the pieces of the ship my parents gave me. I owe them, and everyone on the ship, to go home and tell the authorities what happened."

Chapter 9

Acceptance of the Inevitable

"I don't trust, Anders."

His face fell, and his gaze dropped to the floor again. "I will leave. But can I ask you not to reveal my secret until I have left? You are the first person I have told since Mr. Reed."

Mere closed the distance between them and held a hand to his cheek. "I don't mean I don't trust you. I mean, life has taught me not to trust anyone. And you lied to me."

It hurt even more since they'd slept together. She pushed away the memories of Tyson. The situations were completely different. A large part of her understood exactly why Anders had lied. Tyson had no excuse except for being a privileged asshole.

"I am sorry. I did not mean for things to go as far as they did."

"Thank you for the apology. And I don't know what you could have said. I wouldn't have believed you if I hadn't seen your blood."

"I believe this is what you call a rock and a hard place."

Mere grinned halfheartedly. "Yes. Or damned if you do and

46

damned if you don't."

He returned the grin, sadness dulling his usually bright eyes. "I will leave if you want me to. I have no desire to hurt you more."

She sighed. "I need some time. I will keep your secret, though. After what the government did to your parents, it's the least I can do. And please come by the library soon to look for Mr. Reed's will. There might be a clue to what happened to your gadgets."

He met her gaze, and hope flared in his face. Mere needed to quash it before something else happened.

"I'm not saying I forgive you, but I understand why you did what you did. And since your plans don't include staying here, it will be a moot point before long. You have my silence and my help. Please don't ask any more from me."

Another emotion flashed. Disappointment, maybe. Acceptance of the inevitable, probably. He broke eye contact too quickly for her to tell.

"Thank you, Meretta. I will come by on Wednesday, if that suits you. I know Tuesdays are busy."

He walked down the hall, his feet thudding softly on the tile floor. The bedroom door shut and Mere collapsed onto a chair, cradling her head in her hands. What the hell had she gotten herself into?

Tyson had lured her in with extravagant dates and beautiful things a year after she graduated college. They met at a fundraiser for the school she worked at. She believed he was a businessman with a heart of gold. Turned out he was a scion of a wealthy family who had no heart whatsoever.

He'd worked hard to isolate her from her friends and family, and once he'd accomplished that, Tyson turned violent. Well, he hadn't *turned* violent. He'd merely stopped hiding his true nature. Alone, she saw no way out. She hid away the bruises. Then five years and some change ago, a social worker had run a professional development at the school about how to spot signs of domestic abuse and the available resources.

The next time Ty went out of town on business, she left.

He'd taken her trust and sent it through the garbage disposal. And as soon as she trusted someone outside her family and old friends again, it turned out he was a liar, too.

But Anders hadn't tried to control her. Not her body, not her mind, not her heart. Anders had only asked she keep his secret. No threats, no change to his voice or his body language. And he seemed more than willing to accept she might never forgive him.

The door to the bedroom rattled, and Anders emerged, fully dressed, with his boots on. Damn, he was a fine-looking ma— alien.

"Thank you for understanding." Emotion thickened his voice.

"Thank you for respecting my need for space."

Anders nodded and slipped out the front door.

"Oh, hello young man." Auntie Nay's voice wafted through the door.

Mere dropped her head to the table and muttered, "Crap."

"Hello, ma'am."

"Nice morning."

"It is. Have a nice day."

His footsteps faded and Nadine burst into the house.

"Don't start, Auntie." Mere left her head where it was.

"Please tell me you got yourself some of that."

She groaned into the crook of her arm, not wanting to talk about her sex life with her great-aunt. But once she got hold of an idea, Nadine hung on like a Gila monster.

Aunt Nadine snagged Mere's coffee cup and refilled it, as well as her own. The liquid sloshed out, leaving a wet ring.

"It was that bad?" Though there was a hint of laughter in her aunt's voice, concern was the major note.

Mere lifted her head. Nadine peered over the edge of her mug as she sipped.

"No." Mere picked up her mug and savored a mouthful. "But I shouldn't have done it."

"No more beating yourself up over old what's-his-name. Someone as easy on the eyes as Anders should wash away the taste of any other jerk from your past."

It had. *He* had. And yet…

"He's only in town for a bit, and we're not a good fit."

"Honey, you know *things* stretch, right?" She made a gesture to her nether region.

The heat flowed through her face and Mere moaned. She put her head back down on the table.

"Thanks for the visual. And that's not what I meant."

Her aunt's chuckle filled the room, chasing away the pity party. "Oh, Mere. You're only young once. Enjoy this. I wish I had when I was your age."

Mere raised her gaze, glancing over her arms. "But you didn't make a mistake like mine."

"Nope. I made my own. Regretted many of them, but I learned from all of them. Maybe you learned the wrong thing from your last relationship."

Glaring at her aunt, Mere sipped her coffee with furious intent.

"Don't give me that look," Nadine said from behind her own mug. "If you had learned the right lesson, you'd have been dating by now, not hooking up with the stranger in town."

"Auntie…" A warning threaded through the word.

"You are going to hear me out, then I promise to never mention it again."

Mere drank her coffee and said nothing. Long experience told her Nadine would ignore her objection. At least her aunt was always true to her word. If she got through this lecture, it would be the end of the discussion.

"You learned to distrust. It's one of the hardest lessons anyone has to learn, and I'm sorry beyond anything you had to learn it the way you did. But what you should have learned is there are people worth trusting. You came home and your mom and dad took you in, gave you the safety you needed. You trusted them. You trusted me. You've learned to trust the people at the library. But you haven't tried to trust anyone outside your little circle."

She hated how accurate her aunt's summary was, and hated how the only answer she had at the moment was a glower over the kitchen table. But Nadine was made of sterner stuff than anyone ever gave her credit for. She ignored Mere's expression and kept going.

"Now, I don't know if Anders is the right person, but neither will you if you don't give him a chance. Kicking him out after one night isn't giving him a chance. And, even more important, it's not giving you one either. Capiche?"

Mere grunted, and Nadine smiled smugly, taking that as a tick in her win column. Frustration threaded its wiggly wire through her mood. If she could tell Nadine even part of the truth, her aunt would understand. But even that seemed a betrayal of Anders's trust. And as much as she didn't trust him yet, she was honored he'd trusted her. She'd go a long way to protect his secret.

"I will take your words under advisement," she muttered.

Aunt Nadine patted her shoulder and rose to leave. "That's my girl. And if you change your mind, the Walmart has the best selection of condoms in the county."

Mere stuck her fingers in her ears and hummed loudly as her aunt marched proudly to her side of the duplex.

Chapter 10
Melted Butter

True to his word, Anders strolled through the library door right after lunch on Wednesday. God, he'd never looked so good. What was wrong with her?

He moseyed over—it almost had her drooling, the way his muscles shifted under his jeans, reminding her of how they'd felt under her fingers. Dee looked from Mere to Anders and back again, a grin spreading over her face.

"I'll just…" She disappeared into the stacks with a book cart.

Mere barely heard her, her entire being focused upon Anders, as if he was the center of her universe. Maybe he was, dammit, if only for a little longer, but he didn't need to know that.

"Good afternoon, Meretta." His voice curled through her like melted butter, liquid warmth settling low in her belly.

She bit her lip and took a deep breath through her nose, trying to calm the instinct that wanted to grab him by the shirt and kiss his sexy grin right off.

"Hey, Anders," she muttered, the heat washing up her neck and settling across her cheeks and nose.

The damn grin only widened, as though he could sense exactly how she reacted to him.

"Were you able to look for those documents?" he asked when she said nothing else.

Mere mumbled something about being right back before she scurried off and slipped through the door to the basement. She had, indeed, looked through the old wills and found Mr. Reed's this morning when it had been slow. Digging further, Mere had also found property deeds and a few blueprints for additions to the house.

All the documents fit easily into a small box, and she emerged triumphant from the basement door a few minutes later. Anders sat at his usual table. Dee still patrolled the stacks, but a volunteer manned the checkout counter. With the self-check computers, though, he was mostly there to fetch her should anyone have issues. It was quiet after lunch and before school let out, the perfect time for the archive librarian to help a patron with complicated historical documents.

Mere took a seat next to Anders, the heat of his body easily traversing the few inches between them and warming her, reminding her of how warm his skin was. Would it be the same in his natural form? How would his scaly skin feel under her fingertips?

He cleared his throat and arched a brow at her, pulling her away from the decidedly erotic and unprofessional thoughts about him. His grin returned, all-knowing and irritating as hell.

"What are you thinking, Meretta?" His voice thrummed a string leading straight to the tightening place deep inside, the one only he could release.

Her voice failed her, and she shook her head. No way was she going to answer that question. He chuckled, which only increased the tension.

"Do you want my help, or do you want to tease me?" Her words were supposed to have a bite, but they came out choked.

The smile flattened, but his eyes still twinkled in the way they always had. And now that she reflected on it, the description was apt.

"I would very much appreciate your help, Ms. Larsen."

She took a moment while she arranged the papers in front of him to regain her composure. It wasn't easy—having him so close was a class-A distraction all its own—but her excitement at what she might have found leveled that up a couple of notches.

"Look at this first." She pointed at the will.

Mr. Reed had left his house and the surrounding few acres to his son, which was the property Anders lived on now. But he'd split the remaining acreage between his two daughters. If Mr. Reed hid the alien gizmos, there were three places they could be.

"What's on the other properties?"

Mere smiled and pulled out the property documents. Anders helped her unroll the paper, and they weighed down the edges with books. The daughters had built their own homes after their father's death, and their brother had sold the original property three decades later. The new owner must be Anders's landlord.

Anders frowned as he peered at the documents. "These houses are too new, but the lean-to...I remember it now. Mr. Reed had me hide there when they were looking for me. It was close to the forest and out of sight of the house and the barn."

"Could be worth investigating," she said. "There's also this."

She pulled out the blueprints to the Reed house. And the blueprints for several additions both Mr. Reed and his son had received permits for. Mere would have to ask her aunt, but from the little she'd gleaned from pulling the documents, the house had remained relatively unchanged in the decades since. Mr. Reed had added an extra room a few years before he died, perhaps around the time Anders had stayed with him. His son had added a full garage and a new guest suite.

"If I was going to hide something important and secret, I might put it in a wall." Mere pointed to the date on the blueprint of the last addition Mr. Reed had overseen. "Wasn't this the year you...visited?"

"No, I arrived two years before, I think. My idea of time here was muddled at first. He could have stashed the device somewhere and hid it better later, especially since I failed to return as quickly as either of us expected."

"Sounds like you have some places to look now."

"But how am I supposed to look through walls?"

Mere rolled her eyes. "Was it made of metal?"

He nodded and his brows rose. "Stud finder."

She held in the snicker that term always caused. He caught the pained looked and cocked an eyebrow at her.

"Thank you. Can I make copies of these documents?"

She bit her lip. "I have to make the copies since they're official documents, and the blueprints have to be copied on a special machine. I'll have to charge you."

"Of course, Ms. Larsen." He tipped his hat. "Much obliged."

Mere resisted the temptation to swat him for his old-fashioned formality.

CHAPTER 11
Black SUV

Two days later, Mere was beyond curious about how Anders's search had turned out, but she hadn't seen or heard from him since Wednesday. Not that she blamed him. She had asked for space, and he was giving it to her. She would have to make the next move if she wanted anything else from their budding relationship.

As she drove up to the library, a shiver ran down her spine. Parked in her spot was a black SUV with government plates. Oh boy, this wasn't good. She parked and took a moment to gather her things, clenching her hands to still their shaking. Although it could be about anything, the likelihood it was about Anders was close to one hundred percent.

Mere exited her vehicle and approached the door of the library. Both front doors of the SUV opened, and two people emerged. The woman was taller than the man, but both wore dark suits and sensible shoes.

"Good morning. Are you the librarian?" the woman asked with a cool, professional smile.

Her partner didn't smile at all. His gaze scanned the area

and his hand hovered too close to his firearm on his hip for Mere's comfort.

She played along. What other choice did she have if she wanted to keep Anders safe?

"Good morning. I am. What can I do for you?"

Mere fumbled with the lock and hoped they'd chalk it up to overall nervousness in dealing with armed government officials.

"I'm Special Agent Gaudin and this is Special Agent Okabe. We have questions about some irregular internet usage here at your library." The man spoke this time, his tone clipped and icy.

"That sounds serious," Mere said noncommittally. It could be, but why would they send special agents to investigate irregular internet usage? What the hell did "irregular internet usage" mean, anyway? *Keep calm.*

"Yes, it can be."

"Well, come on in."

Mere held the door open for the agents and kept her breathing smooth and even. Panicking would help exactly no one. She let the door close behind her, but decided not to relock it the way she usually did. It would be bad enough if she ended up needing a quick exit; it would be so much worse if she had to pull her keys out first.

She strode to the circulation desk. "Give me a minute to put away my things, and you'll have my undivided attention until we open."

Which would be in thirty minutes. How much trouble could she get into in thirty minutes?

Tucking her purse into the locked filing cabinet and placing her coffee cup on her desk, she flipped on the light switch. Mere plastered on her best fake smile and faced the agents. They were so close she wouldn't have to extend her arm fully to touch Special Agent Okabe. Her smile faltered.

At this, Special Agent Gaudin finally cracked a small, cruel smile of his own.

"We need to see your computer logs," he demanded.

"Sure. Show me your warrant, court order, or whatever, and I'll be happy to show you." She forced the smile to return and prayed it wasn't a grimace.

Special Agent Okabe blinked. "You have no idea what is at stake, Ms. Larsen."

Mere dropped the smile. "You're right, but I understand my obligations to our patrons' confidentiality. We're a government agency, and I will certainly abide by the law, which says you need a legal order for me to turn over any of that information."

"We can confiscate it now," the man said as his hand drifted close to his gun once more.

Okabe nudged him with her elbow. "Then we wouldn't be able to use it in a court of law, Gaudin."

"Like it matters," he muttered, but his arm fell to his side and his threatening posture relaxed.

Mere doubted she was supposed to hear the last part, so she ignored it.

"We'll bring a warrant by later," Okabe said, all professional once more.

"Is there anything else I can help you with in the meantime?" Mere held her breath.

Gaudin studied her through narrowed eyes. After a moment's silence and just as Mere wasn't sure how much longer she could withstand his stare without squirming, he spoke.

"Notice anyone odd hanging around?"

A half-grin twitched up the corner of her mouth and her shoulders relaxed. "It's a library. We're a magnet for odd."

The man clenched his jaw and glowered. She'd made him mad. The woman placed a hand on his shoulder and took over the questioning.

"Anyone stand out?"

"No," she lied.

"Have there been any unusual document requests?" The ice in Okabe's voice melted a little now that Mere was cooperating.

Crap. If she lied this time, they'd find out as soon as they had a court order. And that would raise eyebrows. Why lie if she had nothing to hide? She went with a version of the truth.

"A few. To be honest, besides copies of birth and death certificates, marriage licenses, and divorce decrees, any request is a little unusual. But I still can't tell you who requested it."

"We'll get the warrant. But what kind of documents did they request?"

Okabe's voice was smooth with a hint of well-practiced authority. If Mere didn't have someone to protect, she would surely spill her guts.

"Let me think." God, she wasn't good at this. What other documents had people requested lately? "A couple of wills, a deed or two, a few blueprints, and a DD214."

They were unusual but not suspicious requests. She hoped that would quell their curiosity for the moment. Mere was just a librarian-archivist doing her job. She threw them a bone.

"If I have time, I'll gather the records for when you return later with the proper documentation."

Okabe smiled and even Gaudin's cheerless expression lightened slightly.

"We appreciate that."

"My pleasure."

Mere stood until they exited the building and then slumped into her chair. Holy moly, this was bad. Even worse, she had no way of informing Anders the US government was looking for him. She still didn't have his phone number or email. She could look them up on the system, but it would be unethical, and it would be logged. If the agents requested those records, it would point a flashing neon arrow straight at Anders. For all she knew, even if she had his contact information, they could have already put a tap on her phone and email servers.

She could drive over to the Reed house. But if she went right now, it would look suspicious. It might look suspicious no matter when she did it, but now would be worse. Maybe at lunch. And maybe she needed to do an internet search on how to look for a tail. Wait, if she was now on the government's radar, could they see her searches? She would have to rely on her memory of spy thrillers.

Hell, this was the last thing she needed. Then why did the idea of seeing Anders, even under these dire circumstances, bring a smile to her face and heat to other places on her body?

Chapter 12

Too Much Coffee This Morning

Mere spent the morning on edge. She jumped at every noise and her heart raced every time the front door opened.

"Too much coffee this morning?" Dee asked with kindness.

"Yeah," Mere replied, grateful she didn't have to come up with a lie. "I should go somewhere for lunch today, see if I can work off the jitters. Mind holding down the fort?"

"Sure, Mere. We've got it covered."

Relief flowed through her. Of course, Dee had her back. The sooner she could tell Anders and return, the happier she would be. Mere had spent a few minutes flipping through an old spy thriller she knew had a great example of evading authorities. She was screwed. They made it look so easy in cop shows, but it took practice. The last time she had needed to make sure no one followed her was when Tyson returned from his trip after she left his sorry ass, but the shelter had kept her safe. Then she moved in with her parents, and the whole town had sheltered her.

Now that was an idea. Would the town help her protect

Anders and give him a chance to go home? She'd talk to Nadine. If anyone could convince the town to protect a stranger, it was her great-aunt.

Mere drove in the general direction of the Reed place. She kept to the speed limit and checked her mirrors way more often than usual. As best she could tell, no one followed her. To add another layer of protection, on the very good chance her skills at ditching a tail were not up to snuff, she parked at the convenience store about a half mile away and turned off her phone. Mere ran through the scrub and ended up breathless on Anders's front porch.

She rang the bell, but silence greeted her. She pounded on the front door and didn't stop until it opened.

Anders blinked rapidly at her, his body tense. "Meretta, what are you doing here?"

Mere pushed past him and slammed the door behind her. "Some special agents came to the library today. They might be looking for you."

The color drained from his face, and for an instant, she was afraid she'd have to catch six feet of muscly man—alien—whatever.

"Were you followed?" His voice was low and harsh but not angry.

She wrung her hands. "I don't think so, but I'm a librarian, not some super spy. I parked over by the BobStop and ran the back way."

A corner of his mouth twitched. "You are one of the most intelligent people I know. Thank you for taking the precaution. Come in. Let me get you some water."

"I can't stay. I'm on my lunch break, and they'll return to the library soon with a warrant."

He regarded her with longing. His hand twitched at his side, as though he wished to touch her. She grasped it, a calm warmth radiating from this simple gesture.

"If they have a warrant or court order, I have to give them what they want. I will do what I can to delay them. Any luck on the doohickies?"

This caused a fleeting grin and he squeezed her hand. He tugged her toward the room in back. Several neatly cut rectangles of drywall rested on the floor, none bigger than a foot across.

"You sure your landlord is okay with this?" she asked in a teasing tone.

"I excel at fixing things. And I doubt he will find a lawyer willing to take on an interstellar case." He smiled halfheartedly and shoved his hands in his pockets.

"I'll come back and help after work."

It was his turn to shake his head. "No, you do not need to become further entangled in my dilemma. You have helped more than I could expect already."

"I want to help." She knew what it was like to feel hunted, knew what it was like to want to go home. Mere had no desire to say goodbye to Anders, but the thought of him in the clutches of the government who had killed his family made up her mind.

"Only if it is safe, Meretta. If there is any doubt as to your safety, do not come."

"Agreed." She let him believe it was her safety she worried about. In the end, she would show up as long as she wasn't leading them right to his door. "I really have to go."

He pulled her to him and kissed her softly on the forehead. "Thank you."

Mere wanted so much more from him, but now wasn't the time. She let her emotions show in her eyes, in the softness of her touch, in her reluctance to let him go. She left without another word.

Her parking spot was still free from large government vehicles when she returned to the library. She'd done what she could and now had a role to play in keeping them away from Anders.

Special Agent Gaudin returned about an hour before closing, a sneer plastered on. "We have a warrant for your computer logs and any document requests."

Dee watched out of the corner of her eye but let Mere handle the situation.

"Certainly." Mere took the paper and looked it over. "I will inform the county attorney and the town's legal counsel, then I'll pull these for you."

A short delay. Anything to tweak Agent Gaudin's nose. He was starting to annoy her, reminding her of Tyson in manner and tone of voice.

"Ms. Larsen, if I didn't know any better, I'd say you were stalling."

"If I was stalling, I'd pull out the handbook and read the procedure to you. Now, if you don't mind, let me get on with my job and you can have your records that much sooner. And you'll need to talk to Mr. Shiratori about the server logs. I don't have access to those." She said it with a sweet smile, but her eyes were nothing but steel.

"Fine, whatever."

Agent Okabe entered the library and strode over. "Everything good?"

"She's delaying," Gaudin said.

Okabe nudged her partner, and he clamped his mouth shut, thank God. "Thank you, Ms. Larsen. We appreciate your diligence."

"She's doing this on purpose," Gaudin hissed as Mere walked toward Dee.

"Let this play out, Gaudin," Okabe muttered.

"Dee, could you please copy the computer sign-up sheets?" Mere raised her voice to ensure the agents heard her.

"Sure. How far back?"

Mere had decided her strategy on the way back from lunch. She was going to be the most cooperative librarian these agents had ever met. If they demanded records, she was going above and beyond to provide every last piece of paper, every last digit. Overwhelm them with data. It might buy Anders enough time to accomplish what he'd come here for.

"As far as you can," Mere whispered.

She had scanned the warrant, and it failed to specify the beginning date, so they'd copy all the things. It could take days, weeks, maybe months to get through it, even from their small-town library. The paid staff was only the two of them, their systems were old, some still analog, and their copier had the habit of getting jammed every hundred pages or so. But they had lots of records. Even with a dedicated team, it would still take time, hopefully enough.

She made the required phone calls and got the verbal go-ahead from her manager and the town attorney. The attorney spoke to Okabe, informing her he needed to be present before any records were handed over. She looked grumpy about it, but he arrived in under ten minutes. He read over the warrant and gave it to Mere.

Thirty minutes later, Mere sat at her computer and downloaded the information called for in the warrant onto a thumb drive as Agent Okabe watched over her shoulder. Browser histories, log ins, and inter-library loan requests. She started Dee on copying the sign-in sheets and other physical records.

"Is this all of it?" Okabe played with the thumb drive.

"No, there's the archive records in the basement. Do you want to come with me?"

Gaudin moved to accompany them. Something about Mere's body language tipped off Okabe.

"You stay here." Okabe nodded toward Dee, who stood in front of the photocopier making the physical copies.

As though Dee would do anything other than what Mere had told her. But the special agents must be familiar with people who refused to cooperate. In this instance, Mere knew any failure of hers to fully comply would result in her sitting in a much less comfortable place answering very uncomfortable questions. And her actions might point directly at Anders. She would do everything in her power to ensure that didn't happen.

Mere flipped on the lights and led the agent downstairs.

"Where's the computer?" Okabe asked after scrutinizing the basement.

Chuckling wryly, Mere gestured broadly with one arm. "We're a tiny library responsible for the archive of the whole county, with records dating to the late 1800s. We don't have a budget to digitize. The county recorder's office keeps all current records on the second floor. These are all thirty years or older, and we only keep analog records of who requests to see them. Sorry. I keep applying for grants, but no luck so far."

She picked up the logbook and took it over to the copier in the corner. It took Okabe a few minutes to realize it was taking an awfully long time.

"How many people request to look at the archives?"

Damn, she was caught. Best to look helpful. "Not too many, but the warrant didn't specify how far back I should go, so..."

Okabe groaned. She put two and two together, but she couldn't blame Mere, who was merely being extra diligent. Mere smiled at her.

"Just trying to be helpful."

"Anything from the past year will be sufficient, Ms. Larsen. If we need anything further, I'll be in touch."

Mere stopped copying. Mission accomplished. She handed over a stack of paper. "Here you go."

Okabe pursed her lips and glared at Mere in the low basement lighting. The agent said nothing as she led the way upstairs. Mere breathed her first sigh of relief since she pulled into the parking lot this morning as she watched the agents leave.

Her colleague locked the door behind them. "What was that all about?"

Dee had almost as many ties to the community as Nadine. She would be a welcome ally in getting Anders out of town before the agents caught on to him.

"I might need your help, Dee."

"Anything, Mere."

"I need to talk to someone else first. As soon as we come up with a plan, you'll be my first call."

CHAPTER 13

The Bestest of the Best

Nadine's TV blared through her door when Mere returned home. She knocked and opened the door. Her aunt never locked up until she went to bed.

"Hey there, dearest niece." Nadine waved absently from her spot on the couch. Mere took her usual seat in the matching recliner.

"I know I promised my fettuccine Alfredo, but I can't stay long. I'm sorry."

Nadine's serious gaze locked onto her, looked her over from head to toe, and softened.

"What's wrong?"

Her great-aunt had absolutely the best empathy radar Mere had ever seen. If you stubbed your toe in the morning, she'd feel something was off at midnight.

"It's not my story to tell, but there's someone in town who is going to need our help soon."

"Ah, I wondered why the special agents were poking around."

"You knew?"

"I might be retired, but I still know people. And more importantly, people know me."

Of course they did. Nadine was a fixture in town, always willing to lend a hand, always ready with a kind word or a kick in the ass, depending on the situation. She had been a beloved teacher for decades, and the town trusted her. Gossip this juicy would make its way to her before Mere could even think to pick up the phone.

"Will you help?"

"Did he do it?"

"No. And how do you know it's a he?"

A mischievous grin lit her aunt's face. "I didn't."

Mere could kick herself. Too late, and it's not like Nadine wouldn't get the whole story from her at some point, anyway.

"I can't tell you anything yet."

Her aunt patted her knee. "I trust you. Tell me when you can. In the meantime, I'll get the old lady brigade to delay them as much as possible. Anything else I can do?"

"Can I borrow your car?"

Nadine raised an eyebrow. "You know where the keys are."

Mere rose from the chair and kissed her aunt on the cheek. "You're the bestest of the best, Auntie Nay."

"You bet your ass. Be careful."

"I will."

Mere grabbed the keys from the drawer of the hall table, leaving her phone in their place. It was a small subterfuge, switching cars and ditching the phone, but it was worth a try. The street outside the duplex was quiet and dark. She slid into the midsize gold sedan and started it. Nadine only took it out a couple times a week for quick errands. She wasn't ready to give up driving yet, and she was careful and took few risks.

The drive to Anders's place was uneventful. Mere circled the block once more, just in case the agents had put a tail on her. There was no way her pitiful efforts would fool the highly trained special agents, but at the very least, she wouldn't lead them straight to their quarry's door.

She turned into the driveway without signaling, and killed the lights as soon as she was off the road. Mere parked the car and tromped up the front porch. Before she could knock, Anders opened the door, relief flooding his face.

"Hi," she said.

A sexy, lazy smile curled up his lips. "Hi."

"I want to help."

He stood out of her way, closing the door behind her. Little sparks of desire coursed through her as she inched by, his presence electric. That wasn't what she was here for. In fact, what had happened the other night couldn't happen again. It would make it too hard to let him go.

"I have good news." He led the way into the back room. More squares of drywall had joined their friends on the floor.

"What good news? Your landlord is going to have a cow at this mess."

"I've eliminated this room as a hiding spot."

That wasn't good news. This room had been an excellent candidate for a hiding place. The fact old Mr. Reed hadn't hidden at least one of the things Anders was searching for here was disappointing.

"I'm sorry, Anders." She took his hand and could've sworn a low rumble rippled through his chest. He gently extricated his hand from hers.

"It means the pieces have to be hidden in the lean-to. I was going to wait until daylight, but with someone here to hold a lantern, we can go tonight."

"Okay, but there's no guarantee what you're looking for will be there, either."

He lifted his arm as though he fought the instinct to touch her. It hung motionless in the air for an instant before he lowered it again. His fingers tapped against his thigh, and Mere swallowed, remembering how gentle those fingers were against her skin.

"I know, but if the DNA modifier and navigation module are not there, they are not anywhere I can find them. I am not yet ready to relinquish hope."

"What are we waiting for?" Mere forced cheeriness and confidence into her voice. She was half ashamed of the thrill the thought of him not finding his gadgets gave her.

They tromped through the fields, keeping the flashlight and lantern off until well clear of the house and road. She was glad for her coat, as the autumn air had a nip to it once the sun went down. Ten minutes later, Anders nudged her shoulder and pointed at the lean-to.

The small structure had seen better days. Mr. Reed had sold off the livestock before his death and split the land between his children in his will. No one had any need to check the lean-to in decades. Some of the boards had rotted away and the roof sagged.

Mere swept her flashlight over the ground underneath the roof. A deep pile of leaves obscured any possible hiding spot. She glanced at Anders. He shrugged and swung the shovel he'd grabbed on the way from where it rested on his shoulder. Mere heaved a sigh and did the same with the hoe he'd given her.

About fifteen minutes later, Anders's shovel hit something hard, and a sharp clang rewarded their efforts. She joined him in the corner of the lean-to and helped him clear the remaining leaves.

A large flat rock looked out of place in the midst of the leaves and other forest debris.

"Well?" Anders's voice held notes of confusion and excitement.

"You lift it with your shovel. I'll stand ready in case some creepy-crawly is hiding under there."

Mere pointed her hoe at the stone and took a half step away.

Who knew what was under there? With any luck, it would only be bugs, maybe a small rodent. But a rattler could have made a home under there for the cooler months and might not be happy to be disturbed.

Anders placed the lantern next to the rock and she pointed her flashlight directly at it. He lifted the rock, but it slipped off the shovel and crashed back to the ground. No snakes, at least, and Mere glimpsed a small metal box under the rock. She clicked off the flashlight and tossed it next to the lantern.

"Together." She shoved her hoe under the edge of the rock.

"On three. One, two, three."

They lifted and flipped the rock over, revealing a hole under it and a metal box lodged there like an egg in a nest. Anders knelt and pulled it out. A simple key lock kept it closed.

"How delicate are the gizmos you're looking for?" she asked.

"Too delicate to risk breaking the lock with the tools we have out here."

"Let's head back to the house. I can probably pick the lock with a paper clip or a small screwdriver."

"There are other tools out in the shed we can try if that fails." His eyes glimmered strangely in the moonlight, like swimming pools on a summer's day. How had she not seen he was different?

They replaced the rock and moved the debris around, attempting to disguise their visit. It was an amateurish effort at best, but nature would take care of the rest if they could delay the government agents for long enough.

CHAPTER 14
Put the Kettle On

The return trip took far less time. Mere rushed to keep up with Anders, his long legs eating the distance quickly. The full moon had risen and lit their way with an eerie glow. They returned the tools to the shed and hurried inside. Anders placed the box on the kitchen table.

"Put the kettle on while I find...you said a paper clip or a small screwdriver?"

"Yes." Mere lifted the kettle on the stove, and water sloshed around. She lit the burner and rummaged through cupboards, looking for tea.

Anders returned a long moment later, carrying a small toolbox. He tossed a handful of paper clips on the table and set the toolbox down with a metallic thud.

"I can't find the tea," Mere said.

"I will get it. You work on the lock."

She abandoned her search, picked up a paper clip, and unbent it. Mere watched for a moment as Anders poured the water over the tea bags in two white mugs. The earthy scent filled the kitchen, and the steam from the kettle made the scene of domesticity fuzzy, almost out of focus. It would be nice to have more moments like this with Anders, but that wasn't in the cards.

He turned around as though he could feel her gaze on his back. Mere resumed her task, twisting the paper clip in the lock until it clicked, and the lid cracked open. Something gleamed in the narrow gap.

Anders stood behind her, his breath stirring the hairs on her nape. All she had to do was take one little step to touch his firm body again. Mere resisted the urge and stepped to the side instead.

Anders regarded her, his expression tinged with sadness, and his half-raised hand dropped to the rusty box. He lifted the lid, revealing two small devices. One looked like a smoky piece of glass encased in shiny metal, similar to a smartphone but transparent. The other was a thin cylinder about the size of a thick marker. A thin line of the same smoky glass was set into the length of matte black metal.

"Navigation." He set the smartphone-like device to the side. "And DNA modifier."

He held the cylinder, looking at it with what she could only call longing. Wearing a human face for so many decades, he must have wanted to slide back into his original form, the one he was born in, the one his parents died in.

"I can give you some privacy." Mere's voice came out more softly than she intended. She wasn't sure if she wanted him to say yes or no.

"No, stay." He tucked the device into a pocket. "I cannot use it yet. A walking lizard man will draw a bit more attention than I want at the moment."

A slow smile spread over his lips, and she answered with a chuckle.

"May I?" She gestured to the device still on the table. He nodded. The little rectangle was cool to the touch but vibrated slightly.

"It uses the bioelectricity of your body to charge," he said.

"I can almost hear it humming."

"I *can* hear it humming. The frequency is too high for your human ears."

She continued to hold the device. Mere didn't want him to leave, but with the special agents in town asking inconvenient questions, he would have to go soon.

"Now that you have these, how long before you leave?"

His hand formed a fist at his side, but he made no other move.

"I will leave town as soon as possible. But it might take a week or two to integrate this tech with the ship I built."

"Oh." It was the only thing that came to mind, leaving her lips as a sigh.

They stood in awkward silence for a moment.

When he had no response, she placed the doohickey on the table. "I should let you get back to work. You won't get your deposit back if you leave a bunch of holes in Mr. Baker's walls."

She whipped around and took a step toward the front door. His firm fingers closed around her elbow, stopping her in her tracks. He tugged gently, turning her to him. His other hand grazed her cheek.

"Meretta," he sighed before he sealed his lips to hers.

All thought of disentangling herself from him slipped from her mind and out the door. Mere melted into him, this alien man who made her feel safe, treasured.

He devoured her, or maybe she devoured him. His warmth, his earthy scent, fueled her desire for him. She slid her hand under his shirt, and his muscles twitched under her fingers. He pulled her closer, grasping her ass.

Anders trailed more kisses down her neck, lingering at the spot where it met her shoulder, licking and nipping the sensitive skin and sending shivers along her spine. She wanted to rip his shirt off, rip her own off, touch his skin once more. Because it could only be once more. He had to leave, for his own safety as well as hers.

That splashed metaphorical cold water over her. She couldn't do this. If she slept with him one more time, she would never want to let go. And what was she going to do—fly off into space with a lizard man she'd known a month?

"Stop," she whispered hoarsely.

He did, immediately, and stepped away, giving her space. She rested her forehead on his chest.

"Come with me." Anders stroked her hair with one hand and clutched her around the waist with the other. "A few weeks there and I can bring you back."

She stared into his eyes, which reflected the moonlight like a ghostly image on a pond. From the set of his luscious lips to the open honesty in his tone, he was dead serious. He wanted her to leave with him.

A thrill of hope rushed through her at the idea of leaving her past behind. Just for a moment before reality crashed her little party.

"I can't, Anders. My family is here, my life is here. I can't leave them."

His face remained neutral, as though he'd expected the answer.

"I understand." He brushed her cheek with a finger. "I should not have asked."

"No, I'm glad you did. It makes me feel…special."

"You are special. How many people would help a stranger, let alone an alien from another world? You are one in eight billion, and I am glad I had the chance to—"

He fell silent, the thought incomplete.

"The chance to what?"

"To get to know you."

Mere had the distinct impression that wasn't what he

planned to say, but she took his words at face value. She didn't want to go, but their paths were about to diverge.

"Goodbye, Anders." She kissed his cheek, letting her lips linger on his smooth skin. "Safe journey."

"Goodbye, Meretta."

And he let her go.

CHAPTER 15
Out Past Curfew, I See

M ere pulled into her driveway with the moon high in the night sky. Aunt Nadine's head peeked out of the living room curtains, and she smiled. Dammit. A moment later, she strolled out in her bathrobe.

A wide grin crinkled her cheeks. "Well, well, well, young lady. Out past curfew, I see."

Heat rushed to Mere's face. Her aunt's teasing didn't actually bother her, but getting caught still was embarrassing. And why did she think of it as getting caught? She was a single adult, perfectly capable of having an adult relationship or night out, as the case may be, without her family making a fuss about it. And she had asked before taking the car.

"Your powers of observation are once again second to none, Aunty Nay."

Nadine cackled. "That's my girl. Come on in and I'll pour us a nightcap. Give me the dirty details and I promise not to tell your mother."

Mere trudged up the steps, but her footfalls were lighter and she almost smiled. Nadine would never say a word about her love life, or previous lack thereof, to her mother or anyone else. She followed her aunt into the kitchen and perched on a chair. Nadine grabbed two mugs, poured a generous measure of tequila into each, and plopped down next to her.

"Well?"

Mere had to giggle. Her octogenarian aunt's expectant expression could have been on a fifteen-year-old.

"Anders—"

"Ha, I knew it. I knew you weren't done with that man yet. You have excellent taste."

"I have to be done with him. He's leaving."

Nadine covered Mere's hand with her own. "Oh, sweetie, I'm sorry. I thought you were a good match. Not only is he sexy as hell—don't give me that look. I'm old, not dead."

Mere buried her nose in her mug, trying hard not to laugh. Her love life was no laughing matter, but her aunt's eternal optimism had her hopeful about many things for the first time in a long while.

"As I was saying, he seems nice, calm, caring. Exactly what you needed after he-who-shall-not-be-named. Wait, he's leaving? Does this have anything to do with those agents poking their noses where they don't belong?"

What to tell her aunt? She could tell the whole truth. Nadine might insist she check herself in for a psychiatric evaluation when the dust settled, but she'd go along with it. Maybe a version of the truth.

"They're looking for Anders. They believe he has a device that belongs to the government."

"Does it?"

Mere shook her head. "No, it's his. They keep trying to take it from his family."

"You're being awfully cagey about what it is."

"I'm sorry. I don't want you to get into trouble."

"If you tell me, you'll have to kill me?"

A sad half-smile twitched up the side of her mouth. "If I told you, you wouldn't believe me."

Nadine stared at Mere in her special way, as if she could see through her protective walls to the soft, squishy core of her being.

"Is he worth it?" she asked after coming to whatever conclusion her superpower offered.

"Yes," Mere said without hesitation.

"I will rally the troops. Take a shower and go about your day tomorrow as normally as you can. I'll call if and when I learn anything."

"Thank you."

Mere stood and stretched, the tequila giving her the warm fuzzies and making her sleepy. Something resembling optimism ran through her system along with it.

Nadine took a sip from her mug. "Did he ask you to go with him?"

She nodded.

"And you said no." It wasn't a question.

Mere nodded again.

"My dear, the chance for adventure only comes around so often. You should grab hold of it when it does. Your home will always be here."

"I don't know if I can go where he's going. He's the best thing to happen to me, and he's leaving. He has to leave."

Tears fell, sudden and unbidden. She collapsed onto the chair and sobbed, her heart breaking into tiny pieces. Though Tyson had damaged her body and her spirit, her heart had never hurt like this.

Nadine's strong arms wrapped around her, hands stroking Mere's hair as she sobbed out her grief. When snot ran down her tear-streaked face and her eyes dried out, her aunt gave her a kiss on top of her head.

"Good. Now, sleep. Your alarm is going off whether or not

you want it to. Your best chance of helping him is to act normal. I've got your back."

With a gentle shove, Nadine ushered Mere out the door. She shuffled to her half of the duplex and did as her aunt suggested.

CHAPTER 16
Windbreaker-clad Underlings

After lunch the next day, the agents marched through the door, accompanied by the town manager and a legion of windbreaker-clad underlings.

"Hello, Mere," said her boss.

"Hey, Ryo."

"The special agents called me on my day off and told me you have given them some trouble complying with the warrant. They brought their own techs to scan our computers."

She watched as a tech shooed an elderly patron from one of the public computers. Mere shook her head. "That simply isn't true. Have you read the warrant?"

He glanced guiltily to the side. "Well…"

"The warrant specified our logs. I gave them all the logs we had available."

"But the warrant specified server logs, and you failed to provide those to us," Okabe said. "I could arrest you on obstruction and open a federal investigation into the town. Corruption is always a good reason."

"Wait, that's what this is about?" Ryo asked.

"Yes."

"She didn't obstruct; she doesn't have access to the server

logs."

"And if you recall," Mere said, "I mentioned you would need to talk to Mr. Shiratori for that information."

"No, you didn't." Okabe's gaze kept track of all the windbreaker-wearing people, but she spared a second to shoot her a dark glance.

Gaudin fidgeted, his hands balled at his sides, and a flush settled in his cheeks.

"Your partner seems to remember, Special Agent Okabe."

Her laser focus turned to Gaudin, and he fidgeted some more.

"Now that she mentions it, I remember her saying something of the sort. Sorry. But she acted suspiciously helpful."

Okabe didn't hide her eye roll and the set of her lips said her partner would hear the sharp side of her tongue in the very near future.

"You have my apologies, Mr. Shiratori and Ms. Larsen. We're still going to have our techs go over everything again. And I still need those files Ms. Larsen doesn't have access to."

"Of course, Special Agent Okabe. Please come see me upstairs when you have finished here." Ryo kept his usual glare for chuckleheads to himself, but when they busied themselves elsewhere, he muttered, "You did give them a lot of documents, Mere."

"They didn't specify the time period in writing, so I gave them all we had until Special Agent Okabe told me they only needed the last year. I called you and you said cooperate, so I did. If they wanted fewer records, they should have made that clear."

He looked at her sideways, the barest twitch of his lips giving away his amusement. "Next time, they should be more specific. I'll make sure to inform Okabe."

"Thanks, Ryo."

"Anything you're not telling me?"

"Oh, loads, but nothing you need to know."

He clapped a hand on her shoulder. "Good. Keep it that way. Tell me the story someday, will you?"

"You wouldn't believe me."

He chuckled and left through the front door. Access to the upper floors was off the main entrance and the only way there was to exit the library and reenter the building one door down.

Dee sidled up to her when a couple techs kicked her out of her comfort zone behind the circulation desk.

"What's going on?"

"They're looking for someone suspicious."

"Anyone we know?" Dee's voice was dry. This town would be considered full of suspicious people depending on who you talked to.

Mere lowered her voice to a bare whisper. "Don't mention Anders. Don't lie, but don't use his name if you can help it. Pass it along."

"Will do," Dee whispered conspiratorially.

Though Anders was a newcomer, Mere wasn't. The town would help because of Mere, her aunt, and her dad. As annoying as small-town life could be, with everyone in everyone else's business, they protected their own. She had asked for help, and Strawberry Creek would deliver.

Two hours later, the techs finished and Gaudin and Okabe went upstairs. Mere picked up the phone as soon as their footsteps faded and called Nadine.

"What's up, favorite great-niece?"

"I'm your only great-niece, Aunty Nay." Some habits were hard to break, even if the matter was urgent. "Were you able to rally the cavalry?"

A sharp intake of breath. "You doubt me? Me?" Her aunt couldn't feign indignation for long, and a low chuckle erupted from the other end.

"Of course not, but things are happening faster than I expected."

"Oh?"

"Yeah."

"Don't worry. I've got you covered. You do what you need to, and I'll throw all the roadblocks I can in front of the feds."

"You sound like a mob boss."

"Thanks! Love you. Be careful."

Mere shook her head at her aunt's joyful foray into chaotic good. "Love you, too."

The clock never moved so slowly in her life. The one time she wanted—no, needed—to leave early, and that minute hand seemed stuck forever at half-past four. When five o'clock finally hit, Mere closed up as quickly as she could. Dee stayed to help. It wouldn't do to leave anything unfinished. No need to alert the special agents she was in a rush to leave in case they returned after she left.

She turned off her phone and drove slowly, taking the most circuitous route she could to the Reed house, once again parking in the convenience store lot. She grabbed the emergency flashlight and thin knit gloves she kept in the glove box and walked through the brush. It was the best she could do, and she hoped it would be enough.

Mere found the driveway of the Reed farmhouse. Ander's truck was gone, and only darkness greeted her. The porch light was off, and not a single window was lit from the inside. Her heart thudded and her palms dampened. She navigated the porch steps; the door stood ajar.

She put on the gloves and pushed open the door. "Hello? Anyone home?"

The distant whoosh of car tires on the road floated on the breeze rustling the trees. Otherwise, silence.

Mere tiptoed through the hall. "Anders?"

Still nothing. She swung the flashlight around. Everything was as it should be. Pictures on the walls, furniture in their proper places. In the back room, the squares of drywall had been replaced, and a five-gallon bucket of paint stood in the center, surrounded by other accouterments.

She made her way to the kitchen. On the table was a piece of paper under a mug. It was a letter addressed to the landlord.

Dear Mr. Baker,

I apologize for the damage in the one room. I repaired the walls but had to leave before the joint compound dried. I left paint and supplies to finish the task and do not expect my security deposit back. It should be more than sufficient to complete repairs.

I will not be returning to Strawberry Creek.
Business has called me away unexpectedly.

All the best,
Anders Haynes

Mere left the note where she found it and returned to her car. She collapsed into the driver's seat, missing his presence. Grief pressed her down and stole her breath. Tears splashed on her shirt, and her white-knuckled grip on the steering wheel soon sent an ache through her arms.

She released the wheel, snatched some tissues out of the center console, and wiped away the tears. She had missed her opportunity, but Anders had gotten away. That had to be enough. After taking a few deep breaths, Mere drove away. Sirens blared in the distance.

CHAPTER 17

Usually a Very Quiet Town

Flashing red and blue lights greeted her unkindly as she pulled in front of the duplex. Two patrol cars flanked the driveway, and a large black SUV blocked the road. Special Agent Okabe stood in the middle of the porch, and Gaudin leaned against a patrol car.

Mere parked carefully and exited her vehicle slowly. No one approached, but all eyes were on her. She walked up the porch steps.

"Good evening, Special Agent Okabe."

"Hello, Ms. Larsen. Getting home late?"

"Had some errands to run." Ice water ran through her veins. How was she pulling this off? "Is there something I can do for you?"

"It's funny, but there were a lot of 911 calls tonight. A few bear sightings, a couple of Peeping Toms, a few suspicious noises from outside. And a Nadine Rask called about fifteen minutes ago with a report of breaking glass in her neighbor's house. Imagine my surprise when that neighbor turned out to be you."

Mere glanced at her half of the duplex. There was, in fact, a broken window. Her aunt had been thorough.

"It is odd. We're usually a very quiet town."

"Yes. And the patrol officers were so busy, they were unable to provide backup to investigate a potential lead in our case."

"I'm sorry to hear that. I hope things quiet down."

A patrol officer walked out of Nadine's half of the duplex, a to-go cup of coffee in one hand and a cookie in the other.

"Thanks, Ms. Rask. I haven't had one of your homemade cookies in a while."

"No trouble at all, Moisés. Oh, there's my Meretta. I was so worried when I heard your glass break."

Mere played along. "I told you I'd be running errands after work, Aunty Nay. Did someone break in?"

"They tried, miss, but your aunt called us right away. Do you have some wood and nails to cover the window until you can get the glass guy out here?"

"I have some," Nadine said.

"Good. Well, goodnight you two. Sorry for the hassle."

"Thank you, Moisés."

He saluted with the cookie and walked to his car. A few minutes later, both drove off, leaving Nadine and Mere to confront the special agents.

"How do you know the patrol officer?" Okabe asked.

"My great-aunt taught high school English for decades. She knows pretty much everyone in this town."

"Fantastic. God, I hate small towns," Gaudin said.

"We have a few more questions for you, Ms. Larsen. Can you spare a few moments?" Okabe took over the conversation again, shooting a glare at her partner.

"Do I need to call the family lawyer?" Nadine asked, all innocence and light.

Mere pulled out her phone. "I don't think I need an attorney yet but give me her number in case this interview doesn't go well."

Had the situation been different, she would have laughed at the surprise on Okabe's face. Nadine texted her the name and number. Mere unlocked her door, flipped on the hall light, and gestured the agents into the living room.

"Can I get you some water?" she offered, as she'd been taught to do.

"No, thanks," Okabe said.

Mere dropped her purse on the floor and sat in her favorite chair. Agent Okabe perched awkwardly on the loveseat, the only other place to sit in the cramped room. Gaudin remained standing, leaning against the wall.

"What's your first question?" she prompted.

"Have you heard the name Anders Haynes?"

"Yes."

Gaudin blinked in surprise. Okabe's expression was neutral. When neither asked anything else, Mere fought the temptation to expand on her answer. This was a tactic they used to get more information from a subject than they wanted to give. She would wait them out.

Silence descended, and Mere reminded herself why she played their game. Whatever she could do—whatever the town could do—to delay these law enforcement officers would help Anders. She bit the inside of her cheek and won this round.

"How do you know Mr. Haynes?" Okabe asked once it became obvious she wouldn't answer.

"He's a patron at the library."

"He's more than a patron, isn't he, Ms. Larsen?" Gaudin chimed in, a smirk on his smarmy face. She wanted to punch him. Mere had never wanted to punch anyone in her life, not even Tyson.

"It's a small town. No one is a stranger."

"Is that why you failed to tell us he was new to the area? We asked if anyone new had come by." Okabe kept her body language relaxed and neutral. She was much better at this than her partner.

"No, you asked if anyone odd had been frequenting the library. Mr. Haynes isn't odd."

Gaudin opened his mouth to protest, but a sharp glare from Okabe shut it again.

"Do you know where Mr. Haynes has gone?"

This she could answer with complete honesty. He hadn't told her where his super-secret spaceship was, hadn't even hinted at it. She was grateful.

"No. I didn't know he left town." True, though that had changed thirty minutes ago.

"You don't buy this, Okabe. She has to know. Several people saw them out on a date."

"Shut up or leave," Okabe hissed.

Gaudin glared at her before stomping down the hall and out the front door, slamming it closed behind him. Okabe returned her attention to Mere.

"We can pull your phone records, find evidence you spoke with him."

"Feel free. I don't have Anders's phone number. We went on a date. It was a good date. I hoped for more." She'd gotten more, but she wasn't about to tell Okabe. "I'm sorry he's gone, but I can't help you."

The special agent scanned her from head to toe with a penetrating scowl. Apparently finding no evidence of deceit, she rose from the chair.

"Thank you for answering our questions, Ms. Larsen. We will be back if any evidence comes to light that you were less than honest with us."

"I understand. Have a lovely evening."

Okabe grimaced and saw herself out.

CHAPTER 18

Put Some Bailey's in It

Mere watched them drive away and waited fifteen minutes before heading over to Nadine's. She walked in without knocking, as usual, and went straight to the kitchen. Her aunt already had a kettle on the stove.

"Cocoa or tea?" she asked her seated aunt.

"Cocoa, but only if you put some Bailey's in it."

Mere grunted her agreement. Her hands shook as she measured out the liqueur.

Nadine's warm, wrinkled hand covered hers. "I'll finish. Go sit."

She collapsed into a chair, the shaking traveling up her arms and down to her toes. Mere was a quivering, tear-streaked mess by the time Nadine plonked the cups on the table. Her aunt handed her a box of tissues and retrieved a blanket from the living room. She draped it around Mere's shoulders, and the tremors subsided.

Mere picked up her cocoa and sipped it. Nadine had added way too much Irish cream, but she wasn't complaining.

Nadine broke the silence. "Talk to me."

"There's not much left to tell."

Her aunt scoffed. "It's not every day a tall drink of water like Anders Haynes strolls into town, steals my niece's heart, and vanishes as mysteriously as he arrived. There's a lot to tell."

She trusted Nadine, but it wasn't her secret. So she told her aunt what she could.

"He's special, Auntie Nay. So special the government wants to find him and keep him locked away. Study him, take away his freedom and maybe his life. There was something his family hid at the old Reed place that could help him escape. He found it and left. He was gone before I got there tonight. There's nothing left for the government to find."

More tears fell. God, how much was she going to cry over another man? Since Tyson, she'd given up crying over anyone with a penis, yet here she was doing it again. At least Anders was worth it.

"I'm sorry, kiddo."

Mere dashed the tears away with a corner of her blanket and blew her nose on a tissue.

"Don't get me wrong. I'm glad he got away, but I didn't think it would hurt this bad."

Nadine patted her hand and poured more Irish cream into her mug.

"I'm sorry it ended this way. I wish you'd had a chance to run away with him." At her piercing look, Nadine continued. "Not that I wouldn't have missed you, but you've been so…"

Trailing off, her aunt merely shook her head.

"Boring," Mere supplied.

"No—"

"Yes. Since Tyson, I've been boring. I was afraid to do anything in case it ended up a shit show like the last time I left home to do something interesting. So instead of seeking my next adventure, I stayed here where I was safe."

"With everything you went through, we were happy you

were safe, too. Your mom, dad, and I didn't exactly push you to expand your horizons. I'm truly sorry this chance for adventure got away, but it's not too late to look for another. You don't even have to start with running away from the US government. Maybe just a quick trip to Vegas."

The rumble began deep in her belly and before they knew it, Mere and Nadine were laughing their asses off. The idea of substituting a trip to Las Vegas for a trip to the stars was ridiculous, but her aunt had a point. She had stayed locked away, ever so careful about her life, never stepping a toe out of line, for five years. Maybe baby steps were better than a great escape.

"Want some more?" Nadine asked later when their cups were empty and Mere had tossed the blanket over the chair next to hers.

"Sure, a little, then I need to get to bed. It's been a year today."

CHAPTER 19
Seven Weeks Later

The waves tickled Mere's toes, and the white sand sparkled in the sun. The turquoise water was even more beautiful than the pictures on the official tourism board website of the US Virgin Islands. She hadn't wanted to wait until she could get a passport, so she booked a flight and hotel for one of the US territories in the Caribbean.

The warm breeze carried the scent of the ocean and rustled the palm trees behind her. Though she wasn't entirely sure how she had found a quiet stretch of the beach all to herself, she was enjoying it. She supposed the weeks between Thanksgiving and Christmas weren't particularly busy.

The trip had been her idea, but her parents and Nadine had insisted on paying for the flight and hotel as an early Christmas gift, happy she was finally breaking out of her shell. Maybe she should make this an annual thing, visit somewhere new at this time every year.

As she walked along the quiet beach, a sense of uneasiness grew. Although she scanned the dunes and the trees behind her and saw no one, eyes were watching her. The tingle in her spine and goosebumps despite the warm breeze told her so.

Walking a few more paces, Mere turned suddenly, hoping to catch whoever watched by surprise.

No one was there. The incident with the government agents must have made her paranoid. Thank goodness once they determined Anders was gone and Mere had no idea where he was, they left town. She had heard nothing in over a month.

She sashayed into the bar and the spotlight turned on her. A novel sensation, but one she'd noticed more often now she had her confidence back. Another thing to thank Anders for.

The bartender, an older woman, gave her a wink. "What'll it be, hon? You look like a mai tai kind of gal."

"That will work, thanks."

Before long, she was sipping the lovely concoction of rum, orange juice, pineapple juice, and a bit of grenadine. Perfect.

A man in his forties approached. "Can I buy you another?"

Mere smiled but shook her head. "Appreciate the offer, but I'm not looking for company tonight."

"Tomorrow?" he asked hopefully.

She sipped again, buying her time to think. This was her big adventure, and she was prepared for anything. Absolutely anything. But she had another ten days, and she wasn't quite ready to be *that* adventurous.

"Maybe."

"Okay. Have a nice evening."

He ordered a beer and joined his small group of friends at a table on the patio.

"You could have your pick." The bartender swiped a rag along the bar.

"I know, but I'm getting over someone."

"There aren't much better ways to get over some asshole than to bed a pretty man."

Mere chuckled. There was more truth in that statement than she had realized two months ago.

"He was the pretty man I screwed to get over an asshole, but it didn't work out."

The bartender absently dried some glasses. "Gotcha. Ever need me to run interference, give me a holler."

"Will do. Thanks." Mere finished her drink and left a large tip, then headed to her room.

She pushed open her door, and the curtains across the room billowed in the breeze. Huh, she thought she'd closed the door before she left that afternoon. She took a step, but movement in a dark corner froze her in place.

"Meretta." It was a sigh, a prayer, a reverence.

Her knees nearly gave out, and she braced herself against the wall. "Anders?"

"Don't scream." He kept to the shadows. "I used the DNA modifier."

Oh. Ohhh. "I promise."

He stepped into the rose-gold light of the sunset, still tall and rangy, with his hands stuck in the pockets of his jeans. His pebbled skin was indeed aqua, nearly the same color as the crystalline waters a stone's throw from this room. But swirls of yellow and blue added depth to the color.

Anders waited in his corner, as he had when she'd first discovered his secret. No threat, no rush, just patience. Mere took one step, and another, until she stood in front of him. Tentatively, she reached out a hand. It hovered beside his cheek. Her gaze caught his, and those blue eyes sparked with hope and desire. The same eyes that had first captivated her all those weeks ago at the library.

Intelligent, gentle, kind. And shining with a light only for her.

Her hand finished its journey, resting softly on his skin. He covered her hand with his and closed his eyes, breathing her in. His skin was softer than she expected, and the tiny bumps had an interesting texture. He was warm, and he was still Anders. Just...different.

His arms encircled her and held her close.

"I missed you," she mumbled into his chest. "I thought

once you had your navigation system and DNA thingy, you'd be long gone."

"Are you saying you did not wish me to come back for you?" The smile was apparent in his voice, though she couldn't see his face.

"No. I'm glad to see you. Were you watching me on the beach?"

"Yes, I was. I—I wanted to make sure you were alone. I am sorry I couldn't come sooner. It took more time than I expected to integrate the original alien technology with what I created using materials and methods here. The first thing I did when I finished was try to find you, but I could not find your number. I called Nadine instead, and she told me where you were."

God bless Auntie Nay.

"Why are you here, Anders?" Her heart raced, and his thumped under her ear.

"Have you not guessed?" He lifted her chin with his fingers. Translucent claws tipped his fingers now, but they were dull, not sharp. "I love you, Meretta."

She regarded him a moment, then grabbed his shirt and pulled him close. Mere kissed him, putting all her loneliness, all her grief, all her joy into this one act. Birds called in the advancing twilight, mingling with the soothing rhythm of the ocean. His sweet taste filled her with longing and desire.

He kissed her back, desperately, tenderly, tasting her like a rare delicacy. Screw delicate.

Mere slipped her hands under his shirt. He was still ripped, but the pebbled skin added a novel sensation to her soft strokes, creating more friction, more heat. Anders yanked the shirt over his head, letting her gaze at him. No nipples. Huh. It made sense.

She ran her fingers over every inch. Anders held still as a statue. That wouldn't do. She grabbed his hand and led it to the ties on her halter top. A grin bloomed on his lips, and liquid desire swirled in his eyes. His deft fingers soon undid the knot and pushed down her top, exposing her breasts.

Anders stroked her chest, the pebbled pads of his fingers sending shocks of need straight to her core. His nostrils flared and his grin turned wicked.

"You still want me?" he asked.

She snagged his belt and tugged him close, pressing her breasts into his chest. Holy hell, that felt good.

"Yes."

And he claimed her mouth once more as she fumbled with his belt. His hands slid under her skirt, the claws teasing the sensitive flesh of her inner thigh. She drew in a ragged breath. She wouldn't last long if he kept this up.

He cupped her through her now soaked panties. "Good, because I want you, too."

Anders knelt in front of her and gently drew those panties down her legs, tossing them off to the side. He kissed up her thigh, and his gaze met hers. Never breaking eye contact, he flicked his tongue against her clit. Mere almost collapsed. She clutched his shoulders with her whole strength.

He chuckled at her reaction but teased her no more. Reaching into his pocket, he pulled out a foil-wrapped condom.

"Will you do the honors?" He held it out to her.

She took it, and as she opened it, he ditched his jeans. Mere rolled the condom over his length. The pebbled skin of his cock added an interesting texture. How would it feel when she took him inside? Her heart quickened once more.

Before she could think too long on it, he kissed her again and rubbed her clit, driving all thought from her head. He cupped her ass and lifted her. She wrapped her legs around his waist, positioning her entrance at the tip of his hard cock, and leaned against the wall for leverage.

Slowly, gently, he pressed into her, filling her, and the texture of his skin rubbed her in just the right way, driving her a low moan from her throat.

"You like that?" His voice was husky with need.

"How could you tell?"

His chuckle rumbled through them both. "Hold on tight."

Mere locked her legs around him as he slowly withdrew and pushed into her again, harder and faster. The texture, oh dear God, the texture of his cock had her squirming in ecstasy. He set a rhythm, in and out, and drove her out of her mind. Their moans mingled in the tropical air, and he kissed and licked his way down her neck and chest until his lips closed around a nipple.

That sent her right over the edge, and she clenched around him, a low sob escaping her. He stopped, and the sob turned into a mewl of protest.

"Did I hurt you?" His voice trembled with concern.

"No, keep going. Please, keep going."

A wicked light replaced the concern, and he did as she said. He exploded inside her as another wave of pleasure drowned her in bliss.

Anders leaned his forehead against hers, his hair—no, downy feathers—tickling her face. She unlocked her legs and he lowered her to the ground.

Mere cupped his cheek and stared into those otherworldly eyes. "I love you, too, An—that's not your real name, is it?"

"No. I was born Zganif of the Qbilit clan." He emitted a series of trills that she'd never be able to replicate. At her consternation, he smiled. "But you may always call me Anders. I have never felt more myself than when I am with you."

"Zag-an-if of the Qui-bill-it clan."

"Close. We can work on it." He kissed her softly and wrapped his arm around her waist. "Come with me, please. I can have you home by the time your vacation is supposed to be over."

She bit her lip, hesitating an instant, teasing. When his

smile started to fall, she put him out of his misery.

"I did not have interstellar travel on my bingo card, but why not?"

An hour later, freshly showered and packed, Mere checked out and met Anders at the beach. The breeze rushed over the waves lapping at their feet as she kissed him. Hand in hand, they strolled to the gleaming star ship waiting on top of a palm-covered hill.

THE END

Anders kept a journal. Sign up for my newsletter and get this free bonus. I also offer several other short stories for free, book recs, and cat pics. Join the shenanigans today!

OTHER BOOKS BY EMILY MICHEL

Magic and Mint Martinis
Contemporary fantasy holiday romcom

Magic & Monsters Series
A widowed witch doesn't need anyone to save her from the
monsters, but one hardened hunter can't let her face them
alone.

Witch Hazel & Wolfsbane
Devil's Claw & Moonstone
Brimstone & Silver

The Memory Duology
How far will Hell's top assassin go to save the angel he was
sent to kill?
A Memory of Wings
A Redemption of Wings

The Lorean Tales
Gender-flipped fairy tale retellings
Blood Magic and Brandy
More coming in 2024

Acknowledgments

This book started as a project in July 2021 as I waited for the publication of my fourth book, *A Memory of Wings*. A few days before *Memory* was set to publish, the very small independent press that had picked it up folded, due to the pandemic and family circumstances beyond their control. This was half-finished, but I just didn't have it in me to write.

Two months went by. I self-published *Memory*, took a breath, and finished this sucker up. But I sat on it, unsure what to do with it. I brushed myself off and published a fairy tale retelling and the sequel to *A Memory of Wings*. I wanted to try serialized fiction but wasn't sure it would work with how I wrote my books.

So, I asked my newsletter subscribers to help me with an experiment. I polished this up and sent out an episode or two a week in the spring of 2023. I discovered that serialized fiction probably isn't for me, but I ended up with the lovely novella you are now holding.

Thank you to the subscribers who helped me figure this out and provided feedback. Thank you to a fickle fate that sent this little nugget on a round-about journey. And thank you, dear reader. Without you, I'd scream my stories into the void, and Edgar (my black cat) truly appreciates the quiet so he can do all the screaming. He is a whiny baby.

About the Author

Emily Michel read her first fairy tale before kindergarten and has been fascinated with speculative fiction of all kinds ever since. She's traveled the world as a military family member, calling many places in the US and Europe home. She settled back in her home state of Arizona a few years ago with her husband and kids.

When not writing, Emily reads, walks, crochets, and pets her feline overlords. Her husband occasionally drags her out of the house for other activities.

Socially awkward and extremely introverted, she nevertheless participates in social media. Check out @EmiMiWriter on Facebook, Instagram, YouTube, and even, dear God, TikTok. If you want to be the first to know release dates, cover reveals, and sales, sign up for her newsletter at EmilyMichelAuthor.com.

Milton Keynes UK
Ingram Content Group UK Ltd.
UKHW012247260224
438492UK00005B/280

9 798224 159192